FINAL WARNING

A CALVIN STEWART NOVEL

JOHN CARSON

DCI HARRY MCNEIL SERIES

Return to Evil

Sticks and Stones

Back to Life

Dead Before You Die

Hour of Need

Blood and Tears

Devil to Pay

Point of no Return

Rush to Judgement

Against the Clock

Fall from Grace

Crash and Burn

Dead and Buried

Where Stars Will Shine – a charity anthology
compiled by Emma Mitchell, featuring a
Harry McNeil short story –
The Art of War and Peace

CALVIN STEWART SERIES
Final Warning

MAX DOYLE SERIES

Final Steps

Code Red

The October Project

SCOTT MARSHALL SERIES

Old Habits

FINAL WARNING

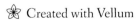

For my niece, the real Lynn McKenzie

ONE

He thought it was one of those wee bastards putting a firework through his letterbox again, until the second explosion, which was louder. Like they were in his bedroom letting the things off. A mortar, or bottle rocket, or whatever the hell else they were called.

By the third explosion, he realised it was the piece of metal and plastic by the side of his bed that was announcing its presence. His bloody mobile phone.

Detective Superintendent Calvin Stewart sat up in bed, grabbed the phone and thought about firing it over to the other side of the room, until he remembered that the last time he'd done that, he'd put a crack in his bedroom window.

'What?' he said, managing to answer it first go. He looked at the clock: five forty-five. In the a.m. 'This better be fucking good.'

'It depends on what side of the fence you're on,' a half-familiar voice said on the other end.

'I'm on the side where decent people are still in their pit,' Stewart answered. How much sleep had he had? How much *drink* had he had, was more to the point.

'Me too, but old Doogie Johnson wants us down here. You included, sir,' DCI Jimmy Dunbar said.

'Doogie Johnson's still alive?'

'And kicking. A young lassie was found behind a car showroom by some cleaners. Doogie has requested the pleasure of your company.'

'Fuck me, Jimmy.'

'I'd rather not, sir.'

'First of all, you wish. But let me finish. I'm half-jaked. I was out on the lash last night, celebrating.'

'Celebrating what?' Dunbar asked. *'If you don't mind me asking.'*

'I can't remember. There were a few of us there. Probably celebrating the fact it was five o'clock somewhere.'

'Sounds good to me. But Doogie's hopping mad like he's trying to get a five-a-side team together, and

he said you're as good as a man short, but he'd still like you here.'

'He said that? Cheeky bastard.' Stewart sat up more and felt the room go round and his belly protest.

'He did indeed,' Dunbar said. *'Superintendent Johnson doesn't normally make it to the crime scene, as you know, but this morning he's made an exception.'*

'Is that the lazy bastard on the phone now?' The dulcet tones of Doogie Johnson's voice carrying on the cold morning air reached through Stewart's phone.

'Lazy bastard? It's my fucking day off. Tell that bastard we don't work on a Saturday.'

'It's Thursday.'

'Aw, fuck. Is it? Only Thursday? One of those twats in the pub said, and I fucking quote, "Thank God tomorrow's Saturday." He was either pished out of his skull or he was winding me up. Wee bastard.'

'Either way, your presence is still requested over at the Ascot Classic Car Warehouse. You know where it is?'

'Aye, I know where it is. I'll have to get a patrol car over. I'm still pished.'

'There's one waiting outside your house. With

explicit instructions for the crew not to knock on your door.'

'I'll have a pish and brush my hair. I might even go the whole hog and brush my teeth as well. Don't say I'm no' good to you.' Stewart hung up.

He stopped short of slipping trousers on over his pyjama bottoms, and managed to get his skids on without putting two legs through the one hole – which had happened before. His brain had alerted him to the fact that his bollocks were being squeezed and he'd quickly googled the symptoms, then within two minutes had alternated between thinking he had days to live and his balls were about to drop off. The transition from Y-fronts to boxers had been easy after that.

Now, by the time he made it downstairs to the waiting patrol car, he had managed to dress properly, using an old army technique of lying on the bed and pulling his trousers on that way. It saved staggering around in the dark, hopping about like he was in a sack race, trying not to trip and crack his skull on the dresser.

'Morning, sir,' said the woolly suit behind the wheel.

'More like middle of the fucking night,' Stewart said, settling back in the rear seat as the uniform behind the wheel showed it was indeed possible to drive after having had a stroke and losing fine motor skills.

The uniform in the passenger seat kept quiet, knowing Stewart, if not personally, then certainly by reputation.

Stewart's stomach growled some more, and not for the first time since his phone rang, he felt a trip to the bathroom might be imminent.

Sunrise was hiding over the horizon, leaving the dark to finish out its shift. The tyres hissed over the wet road and it felt almost hypnotic to Stewart, who couldn't keep his eyes open.

'What way are you going?' he asked.

'Won't be long, sir,' the driver said.

'I was about to put on an in-flight movie, you're taking that fucking long.' Stewart closed his eyes again, trying to get in a quick nap before their destination. Now he knew how his old grandad felt; the old boy could nap for Scotland. But he couldn't blame him. Napping felt good. Though for Grandad, napping meant pissing his pants.

Stewart felt himself slipping away and he didn't fight it.

TWO

'Here we are, sir,' the driver said, pulling into a small industrial estate in the West end of Glasgow. A couple of flatbed trucks sat over on the right. A big sign (which should have read *Robin Bastard Motors* but didn't) greeted them as the patrol car pulled into the side of the road. At first sight, it looked like the second-hand car dealer dealt in police cars, ambulances and a mortuary van, but Stewart realised that was just the team who had got there first.

DCI Jimmy Dunbar walked over to the car and opened the back door.

'Christ's sake, Jimmy, don't make it look like I'm that pished I can't climb out the bloody car by myself.'

'Nobody thinks that, sir.'

Stewart struggled to get his big frame out of the car, but managed it without looking like he was swing dancing.

'About bloody time,' Superintendent Doogie Johnson said, striding over to the car.

'You do realise we're the same rank?' Stewart asked him.

'And?'

'And keep your fucking sarky comments for the lower ranks, ya bawbag.'

Stewart saw the uniform who had driven him there snigger and turn away, which elevated the young lad from *blethering bastard* to *shiftless arsehole* on his useless-fuck-o-meter. Johnson, on the other hand, was still on the same level as a primary school paedo. Stewart looked for a bag of lollipops in the man's uniform pockets, but Johnson turned and walked away before Stewart could spot any nefarious content.

'Where is she, Jimmy?' Stewart asked Dunbar, sucking in a lungful of cool, if not exactly fresh, air.

'Along here, sir,' Dunbar replied. Then, in a lower voice: 'You okay, Calvin? You look like utter shite.'

'My mouth tastes like I've licked the lavvy floor in a motorway services shitehouse. Why did that baldy-heided fuck call me out anyway? I wasn't on the roster.'

'Something about having a senior detective here who would know how to oversee the case, but you would do,' DS Robbie Evans said, jumping into the conversation as the two older detectives approached. 'His words, not mine.'

'I hope his next shite's a hedgehog,' Stewart said, then he saw the forensics tent. 'Tell me that's Fiona Christie in there.' Dr Fiona Christie was one of the city's pathologists.

'You're out of luck,' Dunbar said as he, Evans and Stewart entered the tent.

Inside was Stewart's mortal enemy, Finbar O'Toole. The shorter man looked up as Stewart entered, and they each made a face like a bulldog chewing its own bollocks.

'Fudboy O'Penis,' Stewart said. 'So, you're no' deid.' It was a statement, not a question.

'One more fucking time,' the other man said, pointing a finger and leaving the sentence unfinished.

'Gentlemen, I'm sure we'd all rather be somewhere else, but since we're in this confined space with the body of a young woman, maybe we could move on?' Dunbar said.

'Aye, well,' Stewart said. He looked down at the victim, who had been dressed for a night on the town: short dress, black tights and a lightweight jacket that wouldn't keep a sausage roll warm. 'Was she sexually assaulted?' he asked. His head was pounding now and the cold morning air had done fuck all to help clear his headache.

Finbar shook his head. 'Nope. She wasn't touched that I can see. Unless he dressed her perfectly again, and there's more chance of you being civil than some rapist dressing a victim flawlessly.'

'Cause of death?' Stewart asked. His stomach was rumbling and his head was being belted by a hammer.

'Nothing obvious. No strangulation marks, no stabbing or blunt force injuries.'

Sup Doogie Johnson came into the tent like a Victorian magician, all piss and wind with no substance. 'Just another drunken wee tart choked on her own vomit?' he asked.

'No,' Finbar said. 'There's nothing in her mouth to indicate that, and nothing to suggest that she was a wee tart, you ignorant bastard.'

Johnson was about to chew out Finbar when he remembered the man wasn't on the same payroll.

'Any sign of it being an overdose?' Dunbar said,

glad he had put his overcoat on. Evans, the younger sergeant, was shivering without an overcoat and trying not to show it. The boy was all birthday cake and no candles.

'She's not a user. There are no tracks on her arms.'

'She could have shoved a needle between her toes,' Johnson said.

Finbar looked at the man as if he'd just farted in a lift. 'They don't start off using by injecting between their toes.'

'No need to get your wig in an uproar,' Johnson replied. 'I'm just offering an opinion.'

Then Johnson turned his attention to Stewart, who was leaning against one of the supporting tent poles. 'They're not that strong that they can hold *your* weight,' he said.

Stewart looked at him, expecting the words 'fat bastard' to follow, and that would be all the excuse he needed to lamp Johnson. But there was something feral in Stewart's look that would have warded off Dracula in a blood bank, and that was all it took for the other officer to back off.

'You okay there, sir?' Dunbar said.

'I think I'm going to be –' Stewart replied, and each of the other four men in the tent guessed what he had been about to say before the sudden uprush of vomit confirmed their suspicions. They all danced back a couple of feet.

With very little room for error, Stewart splashed down beside the unfortunate young woman, some of it hitting her jacket. Then he turned away and threw up again, this time in the corner of the tent.

'Fuck me,' he said, grabbing a hanky out of his pocket and wiping his mouth. 'Must have been that bastarding kebab last night.'

'Jesus Christ, man,' Finbar said. 'Not only sick at a crime scene, but *on* the crime scene.'

At that point, it was every man for himself. Dunbar and Evans left the tent, Dunbar commenting that the scene was giving him the boak. Evans looked even paler and took in some deep breaths.

'Keep it down, son,' Dunbar said.

'I'm trying, boss. I'm trying to picture something else.'

'Would it help if I punched you in the bollocks?'

'Funnily enough, I think that would just add to the situation.'

'There's a wee tea van at the bottom of the road. Go and get us both a coffee. And think about Vern.

With clothes on. That should distract you for five minutes,' Dunbar said.

'Aye, cheers, boss. But the "clothes on" bit might not cut it.'

Evans walked away and Dunbar listened to the raised voices coming from within the tent: Johnson and Finbar were taking turns at admonishing the big detective.

'And you can shut your fucking hole too,' Stewart said, blowing out of the tent like a walking hand grenade. Dunbar wasn't sure which of the other men the polite request had been addressed to.

'You should go home,' Dunbar suggested. 'You look like...'

'Shite. Aye, you've already told me.'

'...you could do with a rest.'

'Fuck this for a game of soldiers. I'll be taking the rest of the day off. Tell that baw-heid in there, will you, Jimmy?'

'Pleasure.'

'Right, where's that daft bastard with the funny face?' Stewart asked, looking around.

'Which one?'

'The one who drove me here. He's no' too bad. He had a wee laugh at Johnson's expense. He'll go far, but right now, he's going no further than my place. Catch you later.'

And with that, he made a beeline for the young uniformed constable, before Johnson came out of the tent and expressed another opinion, something that would earn him a prostate exam with the aid of a broom handle.

THREE

Calvin Stewart had gone back to bed, and he was still there when a Roman Candle exploded nearby. He opened his eyes and fumbled about for his phone. He didn't know what bastard had put that ringtone on, but whoever it was, he had an appointment with getting a steel toecap up his colon.

'Speak,' was all he managed to grunt into the phone.

'Stewart, this is Superintendent Johnson. Get your arse into Helen Street right away. DCS Wang wants to see you.'

'Aye, well, I want a fucking Ferrari for my next birthday, but there's very little chance of that happening either.'

'Half an hour.' Johnson hung up.

Stewart looked at his clock and saw it was past midday now. He sat up and found the level of the room spinning had decreased from *fuck me, this waltzer is out of control* to *Jesus, I didn't realise the teacups could make you toss your bag.*

He got up and switched the kettle on before going for a quick shower. Once, he couldn't have cared less if he smelled and DCS Wang had his nostrils assaulted, but now Stewart was divorced, he didn't want to risk bumping into a potential date while honking of puke.

Feeling like he was half human again, he drank the tea. Then, when he was satisfied he had kept the old tosser waiting long enough, he left the house. No driving today. No, that would give them another excuse to take his licence away. Besides, taking the bus would make him even later, thus causing the great one in the office to sweat like a dog in heat.

———

'You're sweating like a dog in heat,' Doogie Johnson said to DCS Stanley Wang.

'It's hot in here,' Wang replied. 'Bloody heating's on the blink again.'

'Bollocks. Just sit him down and tell him what

the score is. Stewart's been rampaging about this station for too long now.'

'He has rights, Doogie. It's not like I can haul him in here and boot him out the door, much as I'd like to.'

'Stand up to him then, Stan.'

Johnson and Wang had come up through the ranks together. Wang had just eased ahead in the game, but Johnson was the one with more backbone.

Johnson always refused to sit in front of Wang, seeing it as an admission of the other man being the superior officer, a thought that had Johnson mentally choking.

'I'll be in my office if you need back-up,' he said, reaching for the door handle.

'I'll be fine.'

Wang waited until Johnson was out of the office before taking his hip flask from his locked drawer. He had just had a wee sip when the door burst open and Calvin Stewart strode in, throwing the door back behind him and hoping it would close.

Wang dried his mouth with the back of his hand and closed the drawer. 'Jesus Christ, do you never knock?'

'Not even before we take a battering ram to a door. Why warn the little fucks? Give them a chance to flush their stash down the bog? That's not what you were doing, was it? Stashing something in your bottom drawer?'

'Don't be silly,' Wang replied, feeling his cheeks go red.

The door did indeed catch and it closed with a soft click. Stewart sat down opposite the boss of the department. Stanley Wang. He wondered if the older man knew he was called 'Wank' behind his back.

'You wanted to see me?' Stewart said.

'An hour ago. Didn't Superintendent Johnson convey the urgency?'

'He couldn't convey a smoke signal if his arse was on fire.'

Wang sat silently for a moment, hoping that whatever medication Stewart was on would kick in and course through his veins as they spoke. Something like a horse sedative would be nice, but he would be happy knowing Stewart was on something that was the pill version of a spa day.

'So, Calvin, I wanted to talk to you about this morning,' Wang started to say, but Stewart held up a hand.

'Let me stop you right there. Only my mother calls me Calvin, and she's been deid a long time. It's either DSup Stewart or sir.' His eyes were wide now and spittle landed on the desk as he wound up the other man.

'Sir?'

'That's better.' Stewart took out a packet of cigarettes and lit one up.

'There's no smoking in the building, Cal...DSup Stewart. You know that.' Wang's heart was thundering now and he was glad the mental detective didn't carry a firearm.

'Do I? I don't smoke. I'm in therapy these days. Traumatised by all the weight I have to shoulder. All the burden I'm carrying because of all those other lazy bastards. The stress has got to me. I'm a shadow of my former self.' Stewart weighed over seventeen stone and would put any brick shithouse to shame.

'I don't make the rules.' Sweat was building on Wang's brow and his right knee had developed a nervous tic, pumping up and down like it was trying to inflate an invisible bicycle tyre, or hold back the flood of urine that was just waiting on the word to go.

'Sake,' Stewart said, flicking the cigarette into the bin at the side of Wang's desk.

'Thank you,' Wang said, looking down at a pile of papers on his desk. Stats from the previous month, his dry-cleaning list, and a suicide note that he would plant on Stewart if he had to ram the letter opener through an eyeball.

Grabbed it right out of my fucking hand, he would say. *Quick as a flash. The mad bastard might have come at me with it had he not taken his own life.* It was a weak defence but one he had rehearsed in front of the bathroom mirror more than once.

'So what's the upshot, Stan?'

'We're putting you on desk duty for the time being.'

'We? Who's we? You and that fucking windbag, Johnson?'

The nervous tic in the knee had been joined by its cohort, the eyelid.

'Not Sup Johnson, no. It goes higher. But we feel that you've been under stress for a while now and maybe a spell at a desk would be good for you.'

'I've never been a desk jockey.'

'You've never vomited at a crime scene before.'

And there it was. Out in the open now.

'Did that wee fud complain?'

'Who?'

'Fudboy. The forensic twat?'

'No, it's nothing to do with him.'

'I bet it wasn't.'

'It wasn't,' Wang said.

'I ate something dodgy for dinner the night before,' Stewart said, seeing a little tendril of smoke coming from Wang's bin.

'I think you have a drink problem. I've asked for a report from your therapist.'

'Ian Flucker will back me up that I've been stressed recently.'

'Drinking on the job could get you fired,' Wang said. *Please God.*

'I don't drink on the job. And if I do have a drink problem, then that's an illness. If I get fired over it, I'll take every one of you bastards down with me. Like the way you have a wee swig of your Johnnie Walker out of your hip flask whenever you think you're going to have to do your job properly.'

'That's enough. Desk duty from tomorrow morning. Indefinitely.'

Stewart stood up so suddenly that Wang had a feeling the suicide note would be interpreted differently.

Super Wang said he couldn't take it anymore and plunged the offending letter opener into his own eyeball. That was the spin Stewart would put on it, he was sure.

'You got it, Stan. Desk from tomorrow morning. After my session with Ian Flucker, of course. I'll have to report this conversation to him. He won't take kindly to me being railroaded by management.'

'Of course. Take whatever time you need with him.'

Stewart walked out just as the flames started to take hold in the bin.

'Bastard,' he heard Wang scream as he overturned the bin, trying to extinguish the flames. Stewart grinned. He wouldn't get the blame for that; he didn't smoke anymore.

FOUR

Fucking Fudboy. This was all his fault. Moaning wee fanny. He'd been a pain in Stewart's arse ever since he had come down from Inverness. Stewart sat at the end of the bar, nursing his last pint of the night. The Stag's Head was heaving for a Thursday night. It was quiz night. Get the punters in, have some old nob read out trivia and the winning team gets to share a bottle of whisky. How do you split that between three or four team members? It was nothing but a fucking con.

Still. Fudboy was in with a few of his pals. Stewart had asked around and found out what boozer he drank in. Trust him to drink in a bar full of doctors and nurses near the hospital.

They were laughing at whatever he was saying. Some young female nurses as well as blokes.

Stewart was slowly getting blootered. Not his usual *pour me in a fast black and give the driver a big enough tip so he doesn't mug me* blootered, but well on the way. The pished-as-a-fart-train had definitely left the station.

He asked the barman for a whisky chaser and added it to his lager.

Then four blokes walked in. Definitely not doctors. He recognised one of them from years ago, some scally bastard he'd put away a while back. Manky Malkie Wilson. They clocked each other for a brief second, and Stewart didn't think the guy recognised him, especially with a pint glass held up to his face.

Five minutes later, Stewart downed the remainder of his pint, slipped off the bar stool and made his way into the cold, dark night. Govan Road was fairly busy as he staggered along towards the chippie on the corner.

What had he planned on doing tonight anyway? Walk up to Fudboy in the pub and start a ruckus with him? Skelp him one? He had been boiling when he'd arrived, and his anger increased when he

thought the little sod wouldn't turn up, but Finbar's
friend had said they went to the quiz night every
Thursday, work permitting.

Now he felt he couldn't be arsed doing
anything about Finbar. He just wanted to take
home a fish supper, then figure out what time to set
the alarm so he could call in sick. Fucking desk
jockey indeed.

'Thought it was you, Calvin, old son,' a voice said
from behind him. Stewart turned round to see the
four men from the bar had followed him out.

'You've got the wrong guy,' Stewart said, hoping
the bluff would work. It didn't. He turned away and
kept on walking. But before he knew it, Malkie
Wilson was round in front of him, putting up a hand,
smiling at him.

'Why are you in such a hurry? You not got time
to catch up with some old pals?'

'Go away, son.'

The smile dropped and Wilson moved forward.
Stewart headbutted him. The big detective toppled
sideways into a shuttered shop window as Wilson
fell. Stewart felt the first savage kick on the back of
his left leg.

'Let's open the fucker up,' said a voice from
behind. One of Wilson's mates brought a knife

down, but Stewart managed to roll sideways. The knife still sliced his upper thigh on the outside.

Stewart yelled out, watching the steel in the man's hand, looking at the sharpness of the blade that would enter him and kill him.

Then the man doubled over and grabbed himself between the legs. He let the knife go, and one of the others reached down to pick it up.

Finbar O'Toole stamped on that man's hand, making him scream, just as Wilson turned his attention to Finbar. Wilson stepped forward, a menacing growl on his face, like he was a Pug licking his own arsehole.

Stewart looked up, blood going into his eyes, messing up his vision, but he saw Finbar step up to Wilson.

The small man held a scalpel up to the big man's throat.

'I know more ways to fuck you up than you've had hot soup. Feel my other hand that just went down your underpants? That's another scalpel I'm holding. And yes, I have the manual dexterity to slice you open in two places at one time. It'll be a toss-up whether you bleed out first from having your carotid artery cut open or your femoral artery. Do you know what happens when an artery is opened?'

Wilson shook his head, just a fraction.

'You bleed out very quickly.' Finbar moved the steel closer to Wilson's groin, his hand touching the man's penis as he pressed the scalpel closer to the skin. 'Then you have a stroke, or a heart attack, or if you're a very unlucky bastard, both. Then you pass out, not long before you die. And trust me, you'll be stone-cold dead, lying on the pavement, before your pals have even managed to get the address out to the treble-nine operator. You understand me?'

'Yes.' The answer was a whisper.

'Then tell your pal to start helping the other two and the four of you can piss off. And if I take my hands away and you come at me, bolstered no doubt by the drink you've had, then I will slice the artery in your neck, and then I will take my time cutting your dick off. And who's going to put me in prison? Four against one, my defence lawyer will say. The jury will shake my fucking hand on their way out as we're going for a celebration drink. You got that?'

'Yes.'

Finbar took his hand out of Wilson's pants so fast the man shrieked. The look on his face was one of relief, and Finbar could see him weighing up his chances of having another go.

Finbar held up the scalpels again. 'They'll never

be able to sew it back on again, that I promise you,' he said, locking eyes with Wilson.

Wilson turned to the one friend who was still standing, a weedy-looking skinny bastard who looked like he couldn't fight his way past a wet paper hanky. There was an older man standing next to him, not too big but he had a feral look about him, like he'd been round the block a few times. He also had a weapon in his hand, a black stick, and the skinny bastard friend had a look on his face like he was just about to start crying. He had one hand on his bollocks and Stewart surmised the older bloke had made a connection with his stick.

'Don't just stand there, ya glaikit bastard. Get those two useless fucks up on their feet,' the skinny man said.

It was like a sort of dance, two men being helped to their feet by two other men, in an awkward movement that looked like a sort of drunken ballet.

Finbar watched as the men walked away and turned round the corner.

Stewart was trying to sit up, but the mix of blood and tears in his eyes, not to mention the copious amounts of alcohol he'd drunk, were conspiring against him.

Then the small man was crouching near him.

Finbar's face was a blur and for a moment Stewart thought he was going to get his throat slashed. The man had something in his hand. Stewart wiped away some of the blood and saw what Finbar was holding. Then he felt another sharp pain in his leg.

Then darkness overcame him.

FIVE

Calvin Stewart had woken up in many a strange house, usually the result of a drunken night out, but he had never felt this bad in the morning.

He didn't remember taking a woman back to her place. Didn't remember even *meeting* a woman, never mind taking one home. He hoped she hadn't slipped something into his drink and fucked off with his wallet.

He put a hand down to feel for it in the front pocket of his trousers. There was a blanket. He put his hand under and expected to feel the belt holding up his trousers, but found only cloth.

He turned his head and lifted the blanket, and two things happened at once: his head exploded and he realised that some fucker had stripped him.

He heard the unmistakeable clink of a teaspoon scudding around the inside of a mug before he sensed somebody was moving from what he assumed was a kitchen, and then the figure was in the living room and standing before him holding two mugs.

Finbar O'Toole.

'I don't know if you take sugar, but I put some in. You look like shite, so the tea will help.' He put a mug on the coffee table next to the couch before going over to a chair, sitting down and sipping his own tea.

'Oh, I get it,' Stewart said, his voice a croak. 'You want me to drink that so you can finish me off? Poison me.'

'Suit yourself, squire. I've got the bacon on for some breakfast scran, but if you're not up to it, I'll have some myself.' Finbar picked up his newspaper – a redtop, Stewart noticed; he was surprised the man wasn't reading some poncy broadsheet – and watched as Finbar put his mug down before opening the paper up.

Stewart reached for his own mug and saw two tablets on the table.

'Paracetamol,' Finbar said.

'No' some date rape drug then?'

Finbar made a face. 'Behave yourself. If I was

into that sort of thing, you, my friend, would be down below the proverbial bottom of the barrel. But take them or not, your choice.'

Stewart picked up the tablets and washed them down with the tea. His voice was less of a croak now as he said, 'You want to tell me why I'm in this room with you without any trousers on?'

'Have a look at your leg.'

Stewart lifted the blanket again and saw a white patch on his leg.

'You were slashed in the thigh. I always carry a wee emergency pouch, with a sterile needle and thread in it. You squealed like a wee lassie when I put the needle in and passed out.'

Stewart gingerly sat up and that's when he felt the pain in his leg and a sudden flash of memory came back to him. 'Those bastards jumped me. That fucker knifed me.'

'They did. He did. I sewed you up.'

'A fucking needle? Don't you carry those wee butterfly things with you?'

'I do. They wouldn't have helped with that wound. You're welcome.'

'Welcome? You stuck a fucking needle in my leg.'

'Just as well it wasn't your inside leg. That would have hurt like a bitch. Plus, it would have been too close to your dongle for me to go anywhere near it.'

Stewart drank more tea and Finbar got to his feet. *This is it,* Stewart thought. *This is where the wee bastard shows his true colours and I get my throat slit.* He was too weak to fight him off if the small man took a benny and belted him with a frying pan or something. But Finbar merely stood looking at him.

'Those guys were going to fuck you up,' he said. 'If it wasn't for me and Jimmy Dunbar coming to your rescue, you'd be looking at your bollocks in a glass jar right now.'

'Jimmy Dunbar?'

'It's a long story. Wait till I get the rolls done. You sure you don't want one?'

Stewart thought about it and then agreed that a couple of bacon rolls – no fucking butter – would be the best cure for his hangover. Finbar left the room, and Stewart rubbed a hand over his face and felt a cut above his eyes.

'*That's* where he put the butterfly stitches,' he said.

A few minutes later, Finbar came back with two plates of rolls.

'Cheers,' Stewart said, then hesitated as he was about to put a roll into his mouth.

'Christ, I haven't gobbed on it,' Finbar said.

Stewart ate greedily, feeling his appetite kick in. He washed the rolls down with the remainder of his tea, and Finbar made refills.

'Why does a crime scene tech carry that stuff around?' Stewart asked.

Finbar laughed.

'What's funny?'

'You. Thinking all this time I worked as head of forensics.'

'What do you mean?' Stewart said.

'I'm a pathologist.'

'What? That's not what you said the first time I met you.'

'If you remember, I started to say I was a forensic pathologist, but you interrupted after the word "forensic". Then you assumed I worked with scene-of-crime. I tried correcting you, but you were on a rant. After that, nobody corrected you.'

Stewart shook his head, which made him wince. 'A fucking pathologist? How come I've never seen you in the mortuary?'

'There are a few of us working there. We come and go all the time. Our paths have just never crossed at the Queen Elizabeth.'

'You're not a forensics guy?' Stewart said, like the truth wasn't sinking in.

'Nope. A pathologist.'

'I remember you using the scalpels on that guy last night, right enough.' Stewart stayed sitting. 'I need a pish,' he said.

'Your trousers are on the floor on your left. They obviously have a cut and blood on them. I'd offer to lend you a pair of mine, but since you're such a fat bastard, I'd say the chances of you fitting in them are...well, let's just say you've more chance of getting a Christmas present off a Jehovah's Witness.'

Stewart grabbed the trousers. 'Fat bastard indeed. I might be big, but I'm certainly not fat.'

'All fat bastards say they're big-boned,' Finbar said.

'Right, don't be fucking looking. And we never speak of this.'

'Way ahead of you,' Finbar said, lifting his paper up. 'But just for the record, we piled you into young Robbie Evans's car. He came to meet Jimmy, but the pagger had already gone down. The young guy was disappointed not to get the boot in at somebody. You dressed yet?'

He was about to drop the paper when Stewart yelled, 'Not yet. Give me a fucking minute. If getting my button done and zip pulled up was a manual dexterity test, I'd be well fucked.'

Having managed to cover his wound and manhood, he began tightening his belt. 'Right, I've got them on.' He noticed Finbar had stitched the cut in the cloth together and had made a valiant attempt at getting the blood out, leaving a mark that looked suspiciously like dried urine.

'The three of us got you up here and Jimmy helped me clean you up. You'd better change the dressing twice a day until the stitches can come out.'

'What about the dissolving kind? You don't carry that about either?'

'This is real medical, sterile thread,' Finbar said. 'I don't just carry it in case some daft bastard like you gets stabbed; you never know when a button is going to pop off on your trousers. I've had that happen before. Right bastard that is, when you're on the dance floor and you almost take a woman's eye out with a popping button. I'd like to think it was my manhood that time, but alas, she was a cougar out on the hunt for an unwitting young guy. Two minutes in the bog with my needle and thread and I was brand new.'

'Why do you talk like that?' Stewart asked.

'Like what?'

'Swearing. Calling it a bog instead of a toilet. Aren't all you uppity bastard snobs? You pathologists are all hoity-toity, aren't you?'

'Not where I come from. Besides, you should hear those other bastards when there's no polis around. They're common as muck, some of them.'

'Shoes,' Stewart said, looking around on the carpet.

'Behind the end of the couch.'

Stewart looked and found them. He always wore slip-ons when he went out for a drink. Easier than trying to fanny about with laces when he was four sheets to the wind. He slipped them on and went to the toilet. He came back in a few minutes later, sat back down and drank some more tea. Finbar put his paper down.

'You want to explain what happened last night?' Stewart said.

'You first. Tell me why you were in that pub.'

Stewart thought about lying, but what was the point? 'I've been put on desk duty. I mean, I sit behind a desk anyway, but this means desk duty without any responsibility. Doing fuck all but playing solitaire all day. I was pissed off. I thought you'd made a complaint.'

'So you came looking for me. For what? A square go outside the pub?'

'Aye, something like that.'

'Why didn't you stay sober and wait for me?'

Stewart drank more tea. It tasted so good he suspected there really was something in it. 'I thought you weren't worth it.'

'Well, that's good, because I didn't say a fucking word to anybody.'

Stewart snapped a look at Finbar. His head jolted with pain and he winced. 'If you said nothing, it must have been that foreskin Doogie Johnson. He's always had it in for me.'

'You think they'll fire you?' Finbar asked.

'No. I have too much shit on them. Plus, drinking is an illness. I have a shrink. They won't touch me with a bargepole.'

Finbar sipped more of his tea. 'I got fired.'

'What? Away. For what?'

'Actually, it was more of a parting of the ways. I told them they could shove their job up their arse, so they took me into the office and let me go. But they gave me a severance package. Recommended by the great god we call Professor Patterson. I have something on that bastard, so he was already touching cloth by the time I was taken into the office. He came out batting for me. I gave them a month's notice. That was a wee celebration you saw last night, me having a few drinks with my colleagues. Those who could be bothered to turn up. Some of them didn't want to go down with the sinking ship.'

'What about Professor Duncan "Disorderly" Mackay? What did he have to say about it?'

'Nothing. He wasn't around.'

Stewart was silent for a bit before speaking. Now it made sense why Finbar was drinking with doctors and nurses: because he was one of them. 'Why did you jump in? I mean, you could have just ignored those blokes and let them kick the shite out of me.'

'I saw Jimmy Dunbar come in. I went to talk to him and told him you'd just left. He said he was there in case you did something stupid. Then Jimmy saw a bloke he knew, somebody you two had been responsible for putting away a few years ago. We went out and saw them set about you. I got the first one with a good kick in the bollocks. I was letting off steam. Jimmy got wired in too. It was four against one when it was just them and you, so we evened the score a wee bit. He belted one of them in the nuts with his baton.'

'Glad you pitched in with your scalpel, I have to say. I know we don't always see eye to eye, but –'

'Fuck's sake, don't get all mushy on me now.'

'Let me finish. I was going to say, it was nothing personal.'

'Aye, it was. You slagged me off every time you saw me.'

'Aye, it was. But don't lose any sleep over it.' Stewart grabbed the mug and drained the contents. 'Thanks for patching me up.'

'You don't have a broken nose. His head caught the top of your nose and your forehead, busting your head open.'

'How do you know my nose isn't broken? You're a pathologist, not a doctor.'

'Pathologists start off as doctors, ignorant bastard.'

'Oh aye, that's right.' Stewart was about to stand up, but then he paused and looked over at the small man. 'Why did you tell your boss to shove it? You bored being a pathologist?'

'Nope. They didn't take me seriously when I told them that lassie we found yesterday had been murdered.'

SIX

'Murdered?' Stewart said. His tongue was starting to feel like sandpaper again.

'Aye, murdered.'

Stewart lifted his mug. 'If you show me where your stuff lives, I can make us a brew.'

'If people think you know where my teabags are, they'll think you spend the night,' Finbar said, standing up.

'I did spend the night.'

'I'm hardly going to write that on the lavvy wall.'

'I don't think anybody's going to be interested in whether I know where your Hobnobs are kept.'

'I don't eat Hobnobs,' Finbar said, taking the mug from Stewart and heading back into the kitchen.

'What kind of a man doesn't eat fucking

Hobnobs? What's the world coming to?' Stewart said to himself and looked around the living room.

It was well kept, and obviously Finbar kept up with the dusting and hoovering. Stewart wasn't quite sure if you could eat off the carpet or not, but it certainly gave the impression it had fought a valiant battle with the vacuum cleaner and lost.

There were no family photos on display, the fireplace mantel holding nothing but a carriage clock that had a wee pendulum under its face.

From the look of the fancy cornice work, Stewart guessed the house was old. The light at the bay window was held back by sheer curtains and thick, heavy drapes. A writing bureau sat against one wall, an office chair in front of it. The carpet was a tapestry of red...what? Swirls and loops? Or was there some fancy technical name for a design that looked like somebody had bled out on the floor? While they were carrying a bunch of flowers. And puking.

Finbar came back into the room with the two mugs a few minutes later. Stewart took a sip and started to feel a little bit more human.

'That lassie. Tell me why you think she was murdered,' he said, putting his mug on the table.

'I didn't bring you back here to give you the story.

I know you're a detective, but that's not why you're here.'

'Just tell me anyway,' Stewart said.

'You're not going into work?'

'Listen, none of those bawbags want to come anywhere near me. If they think I'm sitting in an office well away from them, they won't come looking. Nobody will ever know I'm not there. So spill.'

Finbar thought it over for a moment. 'I've no proof, mind, so this is all my opinion.'

'Hurry up, for fuck's sake.'

Finbar sat quietly for a few moments. The only sounds were the ticking of the carriage clock and the swish of car tyres outside as they cut along the wet roads.

'I was willing to bet a year's salary that the cause of death for that lassie from yesterday was a heart attack,' Finbar said.

'A year's salary? Right now, that's precisely fuck all since you quit.'

'Pedantic. You know what I mean.'

Stewart sipped his tea, feeling the beginnings of an urge to go pee again, but he could hold it a little while longer.

'What makes you so sure?' he asked.

'Because she isn't the first. Granted, you lot found the first two victims and handed them over to my predecessor.' Finbar held up a hand. 'I know, there are several pathologists in Glasgow, but I'm talking about the one I took over from. The one who OD'd on painkillers, Henry McTavish. Let's just say, I don't think he went on his merry way all by himself.'

'You think somebody murdered him?'

'I can't say for sure. But I spoke to Henry – I came down from Inverness and had a chat with him on the side – and he expressed some concerns to me. This was about the second victim.' Finbar looked Stewart in the eye. 'My niece.'

'God, sorry to hear that, son.'

'She was victim number two, as I said. Cause of death?'

'Heart attack.'

'Exactly. Just like the first lassie who crossed his table. Henry thought that death strange but kept an open mind. She had no marks on her, nothing to indicate anything untoward had happened, and when he did the postmortem, he found it was a heart attack that took her. Case closed. Then three months later, same thing, and this time alarm bells started ringing.'

'And this Henry McTavish called you?' Stewart said.

'Aye. We went way back. I came down to be with my sister and her husband. I was a pathologist in Inverness, so professional courtesy let me into the postmortem suite. It's busy at the Queen Elizabeth Hospital, as you're aware, people coming and going all the time, so nobody took any notice of us talking. Henry let me know about the first victim, and said he was suspicious about the circumstances of my niece's death.'

Stewart felt his stomach growling even though it had been fed, so he told Finbar to hold that thought and left for the bathroom again.

After an inordinate amount of time, which made Finbar think that Stewart was raking about in the bedroom, the big detective returned to the living room.

'I hope you don't mind, but I brushed my teeth while I was in there,' Stewart explained.

'Christ, I only have one toothbrush. That's fucking manky.'

'Ease up, I used my finger.'

'Fuck me. I hope you washed your hands before you did that.'

'Of course I did. I'm not a fucking animal.'

Stewart sat back down on the couch. 'You think this latest lassie's cause of death was a heart attack. How will you find out?'

'I did the PM yesterday afternoon. My theory was right. Heart attack. She's number three.'

'Who did you tell about this?'

'Two detectives were there observing, but I sent my report in. Mackay asked about it and I told him. He said it was good work, but then I went to the management after that.'

'This was where you then had the conversation about your thoughts? That the lassie was murdered?'

'Aye. I reminded them that two other lassies had died in similar circumstances, but Professor Patterson didn't want to know.'

'He's just a puppet in there.' Stewart looked at Finbar. 'Who else was in the room when you had your discussion?'

'Duncan Mackay. And one of the management team, a suit. Knows nothing about being a pathologist; he's one of those number-crunchers. He went right into damage limitation mode. Told me that there would be another postmortem done.'

'Interesting. Was another PM done on either of the other girls?'

Finbar shook his head. 'No.'

Stewart nodded. 'I think I will go into work today. I'll need the names of those other two girls. I'll look them up in the system.'

'And my friend Henry, the pathologist who tipped me the nod about the girls in the first place.'

'I'll check him out.'

Finbar wrote the names down on a piece of paper. 'My mobile number's on there as well.'

'What time are you going into work?'

'Ten.' Finbar looked at his watch. 'An hour and a half.'

Stewart took out his phone. 'What's your address here?'

Finbar told him.

Stewart made a phone call while Finbar took the mugs away.

'They'll be here any minute,' Stewart said as Finbar came back into the room.

'Who will?'

'The patrol officers. I just called in a house-breaking at this address. The polis will be here in a few.'

'Aw, fuck. Why did you do that?'

'You'll see.' Stewart stood up and looked around.

'You looking to nick my silverware?' Finbar said.

'Posh bastard. I suppose you have a butler as

well. But right now, all I need is my jacket. Unless you managed to make that look like a fucking tramp's reject to go along with my trousers.'

'Hanging up at the front door.'

They walked into the hallway, where Stewart saw his jacket. He slipped it on. 'You'd better stay out of sight.'

A couple of minutes later, flashing blue lights stopped in front of the door. Stewart opened it as the officers got out of the car.

'False alarm,' he said, walking down the path. 'But since you're here, you can take me home. Then you can wait and drive me to the station.'

'But we're on a shout, sir,' the first uniform said as Stewart thrust his warrant card in his face.

Then the second officer stepped forward. It was the driver from the day before.

'It's fine, Mick. This is DSup Stewart. I know where he lives.'

Stewart nodded. The young man had once again moved up a notch on Stewart's useless-fuck-o-meter, to *gormless bawhag*. There was hope for him yet.

SEVEN

If the good folks in Helen Street station thought that Calvin Stewart was going to sneak in and find a little office somewhere in the back of the building and never be heard from again, then they were in for a shock.

Detective Superintendent Lynn McKenzie opened the door to her new office to find its old occupant sitting behind her desk.

'Morning, Lynn,' Stewart said. 'Or should I say, afternoon?' He looked at his watch and saw that it was past midday and nodded to himself.

'Oh. Calvin. I didn't expect to see you in here.'

'Clearly. I see a wee plant on my bookcase over there. What, did they tell you I wasn't coming back?'

He sat back in his office chair, his hands folded over his belly.

'No, not exactly. They said you were moving office.'

'Who did? Old Wankie boy? Well, we all know he has the backbone of a jellyfish. It was probably Jobbie Johnson who was behind this, like he's behind Wank all the time, pulling the strings. You don't want to play with fire, Lynn.'

'I hope that's not a threat, Calvin,' Lynn said, coming into the office and closing the door behind her.

'It's a heads-up. Trust me on that.'

She was holding a cup of coffee in her hand and she put it on the desk like a chess piece.

'I've never had any beef with you, Lynn. I think you're a good detective, far better than I ever was. But those sharks upstairs will throw you out with the bathwater like anybody else who gets in their way.'

'I'm a big girl. I can look after myself.'

'Not saying you can't.' He sat forward, and Lynn kept eye contact with him as he stood up, towering over her. 'You have to watch your back in here, and not from me.'

'I can find another office,' she said.

'No need. I'm going to take over the old one in

the incident room, the one that's been gathering dust ever since old Craigie boy popped his clogs. He's been pushing the daisies up for a year now, and his office is sitting there, waiting to be abused by somebody like me. I already cleared out my stuff.'

Lynn stood quietly for a moment before speaking. 'Look, this wasn't my idea. They told me this morning that I would be using this office from now on. I could hardly argue.'

'I know. They wanted somebody in here right away in case I had thoughts of coming back and taking over. It would be hard for me to come in here if there was somebody in place. It's a game, Lynn, and you're a pawn in it. That's why I said, watch your back. I'll give you a heads-up anytime, but just be aware of what they're up to. When they've fucked me over, they'll cast you aside. Johnson might be the same rank as us, but he's as good as sitting on Stanley Wang's knee. Make no mistake: you can either be their puppet or speak your mind like me, but the latter will get you a one-way ticket out the front door.'

Stewart picked up the carrier bag of things that was sitting on the visitor's chair and made his way to the door.

'Calvin,' Lynn said.

He stopped and turned.

'Thank you,' she said.

He nodded and left. Outside in the corridor, he stood for a moment, fuming. This was what his career had come to, but he wasn't about to roll over and play dead. And he would make sure they didn't screw Lynn over either.

He walked downstairs to Ian Flucker's office. He had made an appointment with the therapist and would not be a happy camper if the man wasn't in.

He went into the anteroom and saw nobody behind the desk. He knocked on Flucker's door, but there was no reply. He knocked harder, checking his watch again. He was fifteen minutes late, enough time to lull the younger man into a false sense of security, thinking the mad bastard detective wasn't going to turn up.

The door to the anteroom opened from the corridor and the therapist walked in with a Greggs bakery bag in his hand.

'I hope you got me a pie as well, Ian,' Stewart said.

The man's face fell as he saw Stewart standing outside his office. 'I actually got two –'

'Magic. I'm starving. I was going to go to the

canteen later, but that food tastes like a dog puked it up. A pie would be fucking rare.'

'Still hanging on to the swearing, I see, Calvin.' Flucker edged past the big detective, taking his key out of his pocket.

'By a thread. I only swear when I'm stressed.'

'And you're stressed now?' Flucker unlocked the door and opened it.

'Not out here, Doc. Walls have fucking ears. Baldy Bastard Johnson would be tossing himself off if he overheard any conversation between us. I'd have to rearrange his dentures if that happened.'

'Well, we don't want that to happen, do we?' Flucker said.

'No, you don't.' Stewart tried slamming the door, but it was on an automatic shutter. He flopped down on the couch instead and put his arms on the back.

Flucker put the bag of pies down on his desk well out of Stewart's reach.

'Crank up your fancy coffee machine there, Ian, that's a good lad.' The line between familiarity and respect had been well blurred a long time ago.

Flucker, having long ago given up any hope of keeping his coffee to himself, turned his machine on and waited for it to heat up.

'Is it that time already? Time flies,' he said to Stewart.

'It is indeed. I know this is going to be the high-light of your day. You don't have to thank me.'

'I can honestly say my day wouldn't be the same without you coming to see me,' Flucker said.

'And here we are, playing the little psychological games that you think you're going to win every time. Maybe put me off coming to see you.'

Flucker laughed. 'Me? No.'

Bastard.

'And here I am.'

'Well, let me get you that coffee, and we can have a nice informal chat over a Greggs pie.'

'No can do. It has to be formal. On the record. We can still have a pie, but the brass have to know I was here having a chat, and that you're under no illusions about the fact that I have a drinking problem, amongst other things. You can write that up, can't you, Ian?'

'It is within my remit, yes.'

'Good. Because you know the amount of times I've been in here, talking about how I was out on the lash the night before. It's a matter of record.'

Flucker made the coffee and they sat down. Reluctantly, Flucker gave the DSup one of his pies.

'You don't want to end up a fat bastard anyway,' Stewart opined.

'Like you?'

'I'm big, not fat. Why does every bastard think because you're tall and broad that you're automatically on this side of an impending heart attack? My other doctor, the real doctor, says I'm actually quite healthy. No offence.'

'As usual, none taken, Calvin.'

They tucked into the pies.

'You think the brass have it in for you? A question I've asked you before,' Flucker said.

'I don't think. I *know* they do. Me puking at the crime scene yesterday tipped the balance.'

'Yes, as finer moments go, that wasn't one of them.'

'Oh, don't you start, Ian. I'll never live it down as it is. Bloody kebabs. I had a dodgy one, that's all.'

'Are you here to talk about your drink problem or your kebab problem?'

'Just explaining the circumstances, chief.'

Flucker finished his pie and sat back in his seat. 'They want you out, don't they?'

'At least try to put some sort of surprise in your voice. But aye, Stanley Wang and his bum-boy

Johnson would like to see the door bang my arse on the way out.'

'I wonder why they don't just let you ride it out until retirement? You can't be that far off.'

Cheeky bastard, Stewart was about to say, but he kept his tongue in check. 'They would love it if I got booted out and lost my retirement. Or a part of it at least. Kicked out in disgrace. They'd love that.'

'You were shot twice saving kids in a botched bank robbery. That should count for something.'

'It did. Once. But I was never one to hold back and I tell it like it is. The job is all politics now. You're either with them or against them.'

'I can only write what I see here, Calvin. You told me you have a drink problem, and I've seen the werewolf eyes on many a morning in here.'

Stewart put up a hand. 'Easy with the *many a morning* stuff there. I don't want them to think I come in pished every day.'

'You know what I mean. However, I don't know what clout I hold with them.'

Stewart balled up the paper bag that the pies had come in and fired it off in roughly the direction of the waste paper bin. His shot failed miserably. Flucker watched the ball of paper roll away in the opposite direction.

'I see your aim hasn't improved much either.'

'I never was one for basketball.' Stewart stood up and burped. 'Fu...I mean, I hope I don't get heart-burn. I might have to get my feet up this afternoon.'

'I know you're pulling my leg, Calvin. What you really mean is, you'll be going to your office and putting in a hard day's work.'

'Aye, that's what I mean.' Stewart walked towards the door. 'Same time next week?'

'Or just feel free to pop in whenever you feel like it,' Flucker said sarcastically.

'Cheers. Oh, and maybe next week you could get sausage rolls?' Stewart walked out and closed the door behind him. He heard Flucker curse. 'I heard that!' he shouted, as Flucker clearly wasn't practising what he preached regarding the use of offensive language.

'And a bloody professional too,' Stewart said to himself as he walked along the corridor, hoping he would bump into Doogie Johnson so he could punch the man in the mouth.

EIGHT

Stewart looked around the office, which had a window and door facing into the incident room. Detective Superintendent Archie Craig had eaten one too many doughnuts and had paid for it with his life, dropping down of a heart attack a year earlier. His office had sat vacant since then, and when Stewart had decided he would use it, he had instructed a DC to clean it, but the young man obviously had the gumption of a dead hedgehog. He opened the office door and shouted him over.

'See when I asked you to clean this place, I actually meant getting a cloth in your hand and running it over the surfaces, like the desk and chair and filing cabinet, not walking about with it stuck up your arse.'

'I did clean it, sir.'

'At least you have the decency to pull a fucking beamer. You still live at home?'

'I do, sir.'

'Thought so. You still get your old maw to iron your Y-fronts?'

'Well, I, er...actually...'

'Stop slavering. If you keep your bedroom as clean as this place, it's a wonder you don't have fucking rickets or something.'

The DC didn't want to point out how somebody actually got rickets, so he kept his mouth shut.

'I suppose you keep the rats as pets too? Dearie me. Lazy bastard. Before you leave tonight, I want you to get your arse back in here and clean the top of my desk. Get the coffee mug rings and what looks dangerously close to spunk stains off the wood. God knows what that old bastard got up to in here, but I'm sure we need to wear protective suits.'

The young detective stood looking at him.

Stewart looked at the computer sitting on his desk. He wouldn't have been surprised to see a floppy disk drive in it. There was an in-tray and an out-tray, and the in-tray had a pile of papers in it.

'Right, son, dismissed. And if you forget to come

in here tonight to clean, you'll be learning to write a report with a pen sticking out your arse.'

'Very good, sir.' The young man slouched away to his own desk as Stewart looked around the incident room. Then he spotted who he was looking for.

'Jimmy.'

DCI Jimmy Dunbar looked up from his desk and got up as Stewart waved him over.

'Tell me this is a post Y2K computer and not some pile of shite you got on eBay.'

'Brand new, sir. I made sure of it.'

'I'm impressed,' said Stewart. 'What I am *not* impressed with is the lack of a fucking kettle. I noticed when I cleared out my old office that some sticky-fingered wank has choried my old one. I need one ASAP. I don't care if you have to sneak in to old Creepy-baws' office and take his, but I need my coffee if I'm going to be stuck in this glorified broom cupboard.'

'I'll get Robbie onto it.'

'Trusting Evans with a job like that is like trusting my old granny to drive down to Tesco without mowing down a bunch of schoolkids.'

'He'll be fine.'

'Just make sure he gets one that doesn't look like a tramp would turn his nose up at it.'

'Will do.'

'And what's all that shite in the in-tray?'

'Doogie Johnson brought that pile of papers down earlier. He said it would keep you out of mischief.'

'He thinks he's so far above me, that twat. It's because his bum-chum Wang got the promotion and not him. Have you seen the way he looks at Wang?'

Dunbar shook his head to indicate that he hadn't paid that much attention.

'Johnson looks at Wang like the boss just shat in his shoe. I don't know why Wang puts up with it. If Johnson worked under me, he'd be cleaning out the toilets and thankful he had that much responsibility. He needs to think twice about coming near me.'

'I'm sure he will.'

'Right, show me how to boot that fucking machine up, and Johnson should think himself lucky he's not getting a boot up.'

Stewart sat down on his chair, making a mental note to procure a new one, and watched as Dunbar pressed the 'on' button.

'Easy-peasy,' the DCI said.

'Nobody likes a show-off, Jimmy.'

'I aim to please.'

'What's the password? And I hope it's *Johnson tosses off Wang.*'

'*DSup Stewart's. Hands off.*'

'I like it.' Stewart typed in the password and watched as the main screen came to life. 'It has the internet, I take it?'

'And intranet.'

'Okay. Let me get some work done.'

'Those papers are stats that need to be double-checked, Johnson said.'

Stewart lifted a hand. 'This is not the face of somebody who gives a fuck about paperwork,' he said, and started clacking his fingers on the keyboard as Dunbar left. He looked up when a young woman entered the incident room.

Detective Inspector Lisa McDonald. He'd known the young woman a couple of years ago and she was a good detective to work with. He was pleased to see that she had transferred back to Helen Street again.

He watched her cross the incident room and knock on his open door.

'Lisa. I'd heard you were back. Good to see you again.'

'You too, sir. I just wanted to poke my head in and say hello.'

'How's old Liam doing these days?' Stewart asked, sitting back in his chair.

'He's doing well, thanks.' Liam McDonald was Lisa's grandfather, who lived with her and her daughter and Lisa's younger brother.

'Good. Tell him we'll get a pint sometime.'

'Will do.'

'I'm in here working on some crap, but I'll tell DCI Dunbar that if I need assistance, I'll give you a shout.'

'Fine by me, sir.' She left the office and closed the door behind her.

Stewart picked up some of the papers off the top of the pile and had a quick glance at them. Statistics. 'Like I'm even going to glance twice at this pish,' he said. He put them back on the desk in view in case Stanley Wang should pop down. Not because Stewart didn't want to be seen not working, but because the papers would be a smokescreen.

He took out the piece of paper from his wallet and laid it down in front of the screen. The names of the three dead girls stared back at him. Then he got an alert that an email had landed. He opened it.

NINE

'Oh, sorry, Dr Mason,' the young nurse said as she brushed against the man's arm, sidestepping around him.

James Mason glared at her as she scurried away. 'It's fucking *Mister* Mason, ignorant cow,' he said, continuing his way along the corridor. Surgeons were way above those measly pin-prickers, he thought.

The hospital looked like somebody had pulled the fire alarm, such was the amount of bodies walking about. Still, he was just another white coat navigating the halls, blending in with everybody else. Not that he shouldn't be here, but this was still better.

He walked into a room where a woman had been

detached from the myriad of wires that had adorned her the day before.

'Mrs Armstrong! Feeling better, I see. Ready to go home with young Ronnie here.' He beamed a smile at the old woman and her old husband.

'I am indeed, Doctor.'

Mason gritted his teeth but kept the smile in place. *What is it with the fucking Doctor thing?* he asked himself. Surgeons were *Mister* because they were so far above those other people. Yes, he'd been a doctor himself, but he'd left that behind a long time ago. Now he was a surgeon with unparalleled skills. The best in Scotland, if not the world. He merely tolerated those other windbags. He knew for a fact that his hands were second only to...well, he couldn't think of anybody better. He could just about walk on water.

'Good. We'll get you out of here today. The nurse will give you instructions and follow up with your GP. You've made a remarkable recovery, but you have to look after that heart of yours.'

'I will, Doctor.'

Mason closed his eyes for a second and pictured throwing the woman out of the window.

'Look after her, Ronnie,' he said instead.

'I will,' the old man promised.

Other doctors thought Mason was stepping over some line by calling the patients by their first names, but fuck 'em. He had more important things to worry about. Like the text he had been sent on his way up here. On the other phone he always carried, the cheapo one. Not the one the police would be able to track him on. They'd all be high-fiving each other in the changing rooms if they got hold of his real phone. It was risky, sure, but with great risk came great rewards.

He left the room and went into a toilet further along the corridor, a one-person affair where he would have privacy.

We need more aftershave, the text read. Aftershave. Code for the stuff he supplied.

Already? he texted back. He knew the person at the other end would go purple in the face at that, but he didn't care.

Yes! Get moving. Tonight.

Mason seethed inside but kept it together. The person on the other end would be in front of him later, and then he'd let him have it. Right now, he had rounds to finish, then he would slip away quietly.

TEN

Finbar O'Toole was in one of the quieter postmortem suites in the bowels of the hospital. It was usually reserved as the overflow suite for when they had a disaster and needed more suites. He had completed a PM on another sudden death, an old man who had dropped down in the doctor's surgery. He had been assisted by one of the newest mortuary assistants, Chris Harris, a young man who had a penchant for video games and smoking dubious cigarettes in his spare time.

'I'm sorry to hear you're leaving,' Dr Fiona Christie said to Finbar. She was one of the other pathologists.

'Yeah, well, it was time to go.'

'I heard Professor Patterson talking about you.

He said you thought that even though the girls died of a heart attack, it was foul play.'

Finbar looked at her. 'I don't trust Patterson. I mean, he's always away doing lectures at the university. How has he got his finger on the pulse these days?'

'I'm always a good listener, Finbar. Come on, let's have a coffee.'

She led him into the office and they chatted while the kettle boiled. Then they sat with a mug each.

'How come three young, healthy women end up dying of a heart attack?' he said.

'I agree. I can see it if it was one, because we've all seen young people on our table, their hearts giving out after playing football or jogging or something. Sometimes they have an underlying condition and it goes unnoticed. But three? I don't see it. I think you're right to be suspicious. Old Patterson has been skulking about like he's a bloody ghost. I've never trusted him. He and Mackay are as thick as thieves. If anybody is going to cover something up, it's those two.'

'You know Patterson was the one who emailed me to come down here with you today.'

'Me too. I think he's old school – thinks women are a pain and just get in the way.'

'Have you said anything to him about the women?' Finbar asked. 'Like, expressing an opinion about the manner of their deaths?'

'I did say to him that we should at least listen to you. They may be in charge, him and Mackay, but they don't own the damn mortuary.'

'Just be careful what you say to them.'

'I will. I always watch my back in here.'

'We have to watch out for each other, Fiona.'

'Agreed.' She finished her coffee. 'Come on, let's get cleaned up and we can get out of this hell hole.'

They started cleaning up, with the help of Chris Harris.

The hospital creaked and groaned as its pipes contracted and expanded. Finbar knew he'd been sent here as punishment, but if he complained everybody would just say they needed him down here, and he would seem like a whiney-arsed bitch. *So fuck 'em,* he thought. One month and counting, that was as long as he had to stick it out.

Then what?

Back to Inverness. Back to his wife and his former life. Irene had understood when he had come down to Glasgow. He had told the suits at the interview that he was now separated and waiting for the divorce to go through, but nothing could be further from the truth. Finbar and Irene were happily married. They had trust, something they had built up over years, and he loved her more than anything. It was hard being apart, but she had agreed with him that there was something iffy about his niece's death.

Especially since he had sent her a copy of the photos. The same photos he had sent Calvin Stewart.

The big detective was a pain in the arse, but Finbar was warming to him. Finally, somebody was taking him seriously. Maybe they could get through this without killing each other.

A radio was playing in the background in the small office on the other side of the suite. The dusty old room would have created a mushroom cloud if it was ever pulled down, but it at least had a working computer. Nothing that would be able to communicate with the Mars Rover, but Finbar hadn't needed to send his photos to Mars, just to Inverness.

He mentally kicked himself for not being more proficient in using computers, but it was what it was. There was always somebody who knew how to use them.

'Chris, you can go and have a break now. There's

nothing else scheduled for this afternoon,' Fiona told the assistant.

'Thanks, boss. Shoot me a text if you need me for anything else; otherwise I'll be in the main suite.'

'Aye, I'll do that.'

Chris sloped off and Finbar wondered if the young man played in a band. He had that look about him: standing on stage, shouting and swearing and pretending it was music, while the audience banged their heads about like the flashing lights had caused them to have a fit.

Chris walked out through the rubber doors, leaving the pathologists on their own. Finbar didn't count the old man who was lying in the drawer, sewn back together again after a diagnosis of a heart attack.

Heart attack.

The words drew Finbar back to his niece and the other girls, young women in their twenties who had died of a heart attack. He remembered back to the time when he had worked on a man in his thirties who had dropped down dead near the end of a marathon. Though he'd eaten healthily and exer-cised, his heart hadn't wanted to play the game and had decided that enough was enough and given up the ghost.

That's why Finbar only exercised the bare minimum. He was amazed at Calvin Stewart's physique; the man had to be around six-five in height and weighed about seventeen stone, but he wasn't fat. He was big but didn't carry a belly around or have a double chin. He was just one of life's big bastards. Finbar had no doubt that Stewart would have leathered the crap out of those four guys if he had been sober. He also had no doubt that Stewart would have had a good go at leathering Finbar, but Finbar always gave somebody a run for their money. Not that he got into a lot of fights, but there was always some big bastard who would want to put a shorter man down. It helped that he always carried his scalpels and knew where to cut somebody for maximum effect.

The lights in the corridor outside the post-mortem suite went out.

'Chris, ya daft bastard,' Finbar said. He looked out through the opaque top half of the doors, expecting to see the lights come back on after the younger man realised his mistake, but the corridor remained in darkness.

'What's he done now?' Fiona asked.

'Turned the lights off in the corridor. I swear to God, if he had two brain cells...' Finbar shook his head and walked away. He'd put the lights on when he left here.

He walked into the old office, thinking that maybe this had been used as scenery in a film a long time ago. He knew the other pathologists were trying to wind him up, but he wouldn't let them get under his skin. Sending him here wouldn't stop him looking into the deaths of the three young women. He just didn't want to drag Fiona down with him. He had tremendous respect for her.

Two cups of coffee were waiting. He took one and enjoyed the taste of the liquid.

'That's us for the day,' Fiona said, coming into the office. 'I'm getting my hair done later. I'm looking forward to somebody pampering me.'

'You married, Fiona?'

'Was. I got rid of him. Waste of space. You?'

'Yes. My wife's a GP in Inverness. Long-distance marriage. I took this job after my niece was murdered. My wife was planning on coming down here eventually, but now I've jacked it in, I don't know what our plans will be.'

'I hope it all works out for you both.'

They were gathering their things in the office when they heard the flaps of the rubber doors closing together again. Finbar thought it was Chris come back.

'Forgot something...?' he started to say, then jumped back in his chair as a masked man rushed into the office.

ELEVEN

Calvin Stewart opened the email and saw it was from Finbar. His first reaction would usually have been to curse the smaller man, but he had to admit, Finbar wasn't so bad when you got to know him. Fucking pathologist indeed. Who knew?

There were three attachments, each of them showing photos of the faces of the dead women: Carol Bennet, victim number one; the second one, Ashley Smith, who was Finbar's niece; and lastly Karen Rogers, the latest victim.

Is there any way you can make these photos black and white? Finbar asked in the message.

'The fuck am I supposed to do that?' Stewart said, looking out of the window into the incident room. 'Lisa!' he shouted.

Lisa McDonald got up from her desk and walked over. 'Sir?'

'You know how to fu...I mean, manipulate photos on a computer?'

'I don't know if we have the software here, but I can send them to cyber crimes, where they have all sorts of stuff. I'm sure they can do it.'

'Magic. I'll forward this email to you with the attachments and you can do the business. Your eyes only, though. Don't go mentioning it to any of those mutants upstairs. Or any of the others for that matter.'

'I'll get right on it.' She wrote down the address of her intranet email and went back to her computer.

Stewart managed to send the photos without the aid of a hammer on his keyboard and felt pleased with himself. He looked at his watch; he would go over to the hospital and have a chat with Finbar. There was no police record on the girls, except a mention that their deaths were classed as sudden. There were newspapers reports, but just listing the deaths. Nobody thought anything was suspicious, which was what a killer would want.

If Finbar hadn't been so insistent, Stewart probably wouldn't have given the girls' deaths another glance. Now the matter had been brought to his attention, he would give it everything he had, just in case there was indeed foul play involved. He didn't hold out much hope, though.

He pulled his coat on and left the office. Jimmy Dunbar was sitting in front of his computer, tapping at the keyboard.

'Jimmy. I'm away out. If Heid-the-Baw asks where I am, tell him I'm doing some research on the stats. And tell him I'm not impressed that he's billing Police Scotland for his fucking golf club membership and that I'm going to ram a putter up his hole.'

'So, just the first bit, then?'

'Aye. I'll surprise him with the putter bit later. Oh, and you don't mind if I take Lisa with me?'

'Considering you're a superintendent and I'm a DCI, I don't think my opinion on whether you can take one of my DIs with you counts.'

'Aye, that was pretty much an FYI.' Stewart looked for the young woman and spotted her at a whiteboard. 'Lisa! With me.'

'You might not want to go shouting in here in case Johnson hears you,' Dunbar said.

'Fuck 'im. He'll be introduced to that fucking putter sooner than he thinks if he talks to me in front of you lot. Baldy bastard. But anyway, look up

Manky Malkie Wilson. See what he's up to these days.'

'You mean apart from getting a posse together to give you a hiding outside a pub?'

'Aye, I mean that. Check arrest records. The usual shite.'

'Sir?' Lisa said, coming across.

'You sent those photos yet?' Stewart asked.

'I have.'

'Good. I need you to come with me.'

'Anywhere exciting?'

'Define your idea of exciting.'

'Walks on the beach. Travel. Sitting in front of a log fire.'

'I said, define your idea of exciting, not read me your Tinder profile.' Stewart shook his head. 'Walks on the beach. Does anybody ever do that, or is that just a template that saddos use for online dating?'

'I wouldn't know, sir. I don't use online dating. Do you?'

'Now, now, let's not overstep the boundary between our professional and personal lives.'

'I'll take that as a *yes*, then.'

'You can take it any way you bloody like. You're driving.' Stewart turned to Dunbar. 'Shoot me a text if that prick asks about me.'

'Which one?' Dunbar said.

'Take your pick.'

Stewart told Lisa where they were going, and they left Helen Street in a nondescript Vauxhall pool car.

'You should really be getting yourself a decent motor, Lisa. It's embarrassing to show your face in a car where some drug squad yahoo's emptied his bag.'

'That's disgusting. If you don't mind me saying so.'

'I don't mind at all.' Stewart picked up the errant chip that had been lying in the footwell, wound the window down and fired it out. 'Manky bastards.' He wiped his finger and thumb on the cloth seat.

TWELVE

The car park at the Queen Elizabeth University Hospital was packed, but Stewart saw a disabled space and told Lisa to use it. 'Pretend we're in a supermarket where every other able-bodied bastard uses them.' He threw the police sign on the dash before they got out into the cold.

They were at what Stewart called the back of beyond, which translated meant the entrance to the mortuary. No matter where police officers went, the mortuary was always the same: drab, dreary and ready to give the unsuspecting the willies. Even in a new hospital like this one.

Stewart took out his phone and called Finbar's number. It went straight to voicemail.

'Come on. Fuck. I'm freezing my nuts off out

here. I'm with a DI. Come and let us in.' Stewart
hung up, starting to feel his anger level rise.

'Maybe he's working,' Lisa said, sticking her
hands deeper into her pockets.

'That'd better be the bloody case.'

'Did you tell him in advance we were coming?'
Lisa looked at him, her nose starting to go red.

'Why spoil the surprise? Come on, let's go in
through the hospital's main entrance. There are a
few brass monkeys around with body parts
missing.'

Inside, Stewart was glad the NHS didn't skimp
on their electric bill as the heat enveloped them.

'Death by heat, or death by cold?' he asked Lisa
as they waited for the lift.

'I'm sorry?'

'Would you rather die hiking across Antarctica,
freezing to death, or in the blazing heat of the
Sahara?'

'I haven't thought about that, to be honest. We
usually go to Blackpool for our holidays.'

'I'd rather die in the cold. Hypothermia would
grab hold of you and then you'd slip away.'

'Just like an old-aged pensioner living off the
government pension.'

'Aye. Poor bastards. They should make all those

ponces in the House of Lords live in council flats with no dosh. Bastards.'

The lift doors opened and they slipped in. A heavy-set man with a bunch of flowers was about to step in beside them when Stewart held up a hand. 'Going down.'

The man looked uncertain, so Stewart stabbed at the 'close doors' button until they gave in and slid together. 'Better taking the stairs anyway, fat bastard.'

'I heard that,' the man shouted.

'I hate it when people earwig,' Stewart said to Lisa. 'So, death by heat or cold?' he asked.

Lisa puffed out her cheeks before answering. 'It's hard to be objective when I'm freezing my...hands off. So I'll go for heat.'

Stewart had thought she was going to say *tits* and was glad she hadn't. There was a line between colleagues that he didn't want to cross. He'd skated close once or twice in his career, and he knew some guys who had crossed it, but he himself had never ventured over and he wasn't about to start now.

'Heat makes you blow up like a Michelin Man. You ever seen a bloated corpse? Skin like a ripe melon that's years out of date. About to explode with one wrong poke of a finger,' he said.

'I have actually. Despite your best attempt to make me vomit, sir, it's not going to happen. Sorry to disappoint you.'

'Old boy, was it? Some old codger who'd been dead for a week and whose dug was about to have at it? Because that was mine.'

They reached the mortuary level and the doors opened again.

'No. Suicide,' Lisa said. 'Big man he was. Sitting on the couch, cool as you like, except the gases were gurgling around inside him and he was like your old bloke, ready to set himself about the wallpaper.'

'Did he take pills or something?'

She nodded as they followed the signs for mortuary. 'Yes. He'd broken up with his girlfriend and had written a note. He also left her a voicemail telling her he was going to do it. She didn't hear it until she'd come back home from a dirty weekend with her new boyfriend. She thought it was a cry for help, and she would have gone round to his place to rip him a new one if she'd listened to the message earlier, but his cry for help turned into a real suicide. He must have taken a load of pills to make it look good and succumbed to them.'

'Poor bastard. Imagine doing that over a woman.' Stewart shook his head.

'Not something you would entertain then, sir?'

'Despite that being a demise that Doogie Johnson would tinkle in his long johns over, I'm afraid not. It's not something I would do, especially over a woman.'

Some people in lab coats walked past them, nobody that either officer recognised.

'You married then, sir?'

'Was. We decided to call it a day.'

'Family?'

'A daughter. She has two wee yins. The wife tried to poison her against me, but my daughter loves her dad. How old's your wee yin again?'

'Alice is six.'

'Aye, Alice.' He looked at her before they entered the mortuary. 'Jimmy told me what happened to your ex. Back at Newton Stewart.'

'It would have hurt more if we'd still been together.'

'Aye.'

Stewart opened the door and they walked into the entrance area. People were walking about all over.

'Busy place,' Lisa said.

'Aye, it is that. They're kept on their toes here.

And when it gets crowded, they keep some of the bodies over in the Royal Infirmary.'

Stewart opened a door and they walked into a lab and looked around at the office over on the opposite side. A tall man looked out of the office window and smiled, then got up out of his chair and came out to speak to them.

Professor Duncan 'Disorderly' Mackay held out a hand when he got closer to Stewart.

'Calvin! Good to see you again!'

Stewart held out a fist and waited for Mackay to do the same. He hated shaking hands with somebody who spent their days touching dead people. Mackay bumped fists.

'How's things, Duncan?'

'A bit of a dead end, I'm afraid.' Mackay guffawed at his own joke.

'If corny jokes were a crime, you'd be looking at life.'

Mackay laughed again and slapped Stewart on the arm. The big detective tried not to wince and vowed to burn his coat out in the car park afterwards.

'This is DI –' he started to say, but Mackay jumped in.

'Lisa McDonald. We've met before.'

'Good to see you again, sir,' she said, keeping her

hands in her pockets, following Stewart's lead in avoiding a handshake.

'You too.' Mackay moved out of the way of a woman in a lab coat. 'What brings you here? I wasn't expecting any detectives this afternoon.'

'I was hoping to have a word with Finbar O'Toole,' Stewart said.

'I think he's busy doing a PM on a sudden death.'

Stewart made a show of looking at his watch. 'No, he'll be finished now.'

'You're not here to get wired into him again, are you?'

'No, nothing like that.'

'I heard about the debacle in the forensics tent,' Mackay said.

'I had a dodgy kebab the night before. My stomach can't take all that muck nowadays.'

'Especially if it's trying to drown in a few Bell's.'

'I never touch the stuff,' Stewart said. *Unlike you, drunken bastard.* Stewart knew he could handle a good few drinks, but he'd never seen anybody throw drink back like Mackay. He could piss up a wall for Scotland.

'Aye, it never touches the sides, more like.' Mackay laughed again.

'Where's the wee man?' Stewart asked, not wanting to compare drinking skills in front of Lisa.

'Downstairs.'

'Usually when I'm in the basement of some place and somebody says *downstairs*, they mean the fires of hell.'

Mackay grinned. 'Not sure that's where Finbar's eventually headed, but there's a lower basement level. Where the overflow PM suites are. The tragedy level, we call it. You know, like a train crash in Central Station or something like that. When we need more room for the victims.'

'There's been nothing like that, has there?' Lisa asked.

'No, but we had a run on some old folks who couldn't pay their electric bill. Poor sods.'

'That's what I was just saying,' Stewart said. 'Just because those old bastards in London have those funny wigs to keep their heids warm.'

A couple of the other staff members turned to look at the big man. Somebody who was bigger and broader than the professor.

'Aye, well,' said Mackay. 'Finbar's downstairs working on an old boy. I didn't realise the time, but you're right, he should be finished by now. If you need anything else before you go, give me'a shout.'

'Will do.'

They turned away and walked in the opposite direction to Mackay.

'Stairs or lift?' Stewart asked Lisa.

'What if we get stuck in the lift?'

'You weren't worried about that a minute ago when we came down.'

'That was before I knew we were going down into the bowels of hell.'

'Stairs it is, but I'm taking the lift back up. You can hoof it if you like, but I don't want any of my organs to give out and then I end up on one of those tables in there.'

They found the stairs and their shoes clacked on the concrete steps as they went down to the next level. Stewart opened the door and stepped into the corridor. It was dark. Instinctively, he took out his extendable baton.

'I don't mean to spook you or anything, but this isn't right. It shouldn't be in darkness like this.'

'Maybe they're trying to save money.'

'I just hope a Nigerian prince doesn't call you up one day. He'll have your savings in a heartbeat. Poor, naïve child.'

Lisa drew her baton just in case.

Light was coming out through the PM suite

rubber doors, the opaque top half diluting watery fluorescents. Stewart wasn't about to shout out and give some nut job a heads-up that they were coming. If it was just Finbar in by himself, then that was okay.

'Being an equal opportunist, I have to ask if you want to go through those doors first,' Stewart said, looking at Lisa.

'Thanks but feel free to lead by example.'

Stewart shrugged. 'Suit yourself.' He shoved one door hard, swinging his baton over his shoulder. 'Right, ya bastard, nobody fucking move,' he shouted.

Then they heard the banging coming from inside one of the refrigerated drawers.

THIRTEEN

Lisa scanned the room, watching their backs, but there was nobody there. Stewart walked forward to the rows of drawers until he got to the one where he thought the noise was coming from.

'Fin!' he shouted.

The noise was coming from one of the bottom drawers. Stewart rushed over and grabbed the drawer handle.

'If this is a zombie, I fully expect you to stay and fight it while I run for help,' he said to Lisa.

'I'm not a fucking zombie!' a muffled voice shouted.

Stewart pulled the drawer out and Finbar O'Toole came out with it.

'Jesus Christ. Thank God you decided to come

along here,' he said. He was flushed and sweat lined his brow.

Lisa rushed over, and she and Stewart helped the pathologist out of the drawer.

'What the hell happened?' the DSup asked.

'Some bastard came into the office there and jumped me. Check on Fiona. The pathologist. She was in there with me!'

Lisa rushed over to the office and saw Fiona Christie lying on her side, blood coming out of her nose. She knelt down beside the doctor. 'Fiona! Can you hear me?'

The doctor groaned and her eyes fluttered. Then they opened fully and Lisa saw the panic in her face. 'No, no! Please!' she shouted.

Lisa grabbed her by the shoulders and held on, looking into her eyes. 'Fiona, it's me, Lisa McDonald. You're safe.'

Fiona's eyes looked wild for a second, but then she calmed down. 'Lisa? Is that you?'

'It's me. You're safe. I'm going to call for help. DSup Stewart is with Finbar.'

'Is he okay? Somebody attacked us. Did you get him?'

'There's nobody else here.'

Lisa took her phone out, called control and

relayed that there was an emergency down in the mortuary and a medical team was needed. She helped Fiona into a sitting position.

Stewart was helping Finbar to keep steady on his feet.

'Are you hurt?'

Finbar shook his head. 'No, a bit bruised maybe, but he got me a good one in the solar plexus and took the wind right out of my fucking sails. Then he shoved me in that drawer. Brought back memories of high school, so it did. That's when I learned to fight.'

'Did you get a look at him?' Lisa asked.

'No. He was dressed in black and had a ski mask on. Black trousers, black hoodie pulled up. Big bastard. I fought him and cut him with a scalpel, but he got the better of me, I'm ashamed to say.'

'It happens to the best of us,' Stewart said, and a knowing look passed between them. 'Hopefully, he was caught on the hospital's CCTV.'

A team came down from Accident and Emergency with a wheeled stretcher and a medical kit. They attended to Fiona.

'I can go and find the security room,' Lisa said.

'Go then,' Stewart said. 'I want to see where he went. But first, get uniforms in here to guard the place until forensics can get in.'

Once Lisa had left, Stewart looked at Finbar. 'You've not been diddling somebody's wife, have you? Husband finds out and decides to give you a leathering?'

'What? Of course not. I'm a happily married man.'

'Where was your wife the other day?' Stewart asked.

'She's still in Inverness. She's a GP up there. I came down here with her blessing. I was only going to be here for a while before resigning. I want to find out who killed my niece and then we'll figure out what we're going to do.'

'What are you doing working down here on your own anyway? There's usually a team.'

'We weren't on our own. We were with a mortuary assistant, Chris Harris. I told him to go since we were finished for the day and he left.'

'Nothing seem unusual about him?'

'Chris? No. I mean, I don't know him well, but he was okay to talk to.'

'Are you normally down here?'

'No. When this place was built, they added this in case there's some kind of disaster. It's only used occasionally.'

'Who told you to come down here to work?'

Finbar looked at Stewart for a moment. 'Professor Patterson. He told Fiona too.'

Stewart shook his head. 'The head of pathology himself sends you down here. That's a bit above his station. I thought Professor Mackay was the day-to-day bloke who ran the mortuary. I saw Patterson more as a suit who sat in conference rooms sipping tea with the bigwigs and pushing a pencil.'

'Aye, well, he came out of a conference room today, all smiles and handshakes, and asked me if I could come down here. They were very busy and he needed somebody he could trust, he said.'

'Sounds fucking fishy to me.'

Finbar winced as he moved.

'You okay?' Stewart asked.

'Aye, I'm fine. I banged my head when he was shoving me in there and the fucker nearly took my fingers off as he slid the drawer shut. I hate to admit it, but I thought I was a goner.' Finbar looked at Stewart. 'What made you come over here?'

'Walls have ears and that fucking station has a bigger pair than anywhere. I just wanted to go over those photos with you.'

'I don't want to talk in here. Maybe over a pint.'

'Sounds good to me.'

'You off the clock yet?' Finbar asked.

'I'm off the clock when I feel like being off the clock. Doogie Johnson better not question me about fucking off out of that place. However, we should let that old bastard Professor Patterson upstairs know you were attacked. If anybody's up to shenanigans up there, then they won't try it again. I'll go with you, then we can see what Lisa found out.'

Stewart was glad to see that Lisa had had the sense to put the lights back on in the corridor. 'Did you switch the lights off in the corridor?' he asked Finbar.

'No. Chris did when he left.'

Stewart lifted his eyebrows. 'Bit of a coincidence, that. I think young Lisa and I will go and have a word with him. I don't suppose you know where he lives?'

'Come on now, Calvin, how the fuck would I know where he lives?'

'Good point. I'll have somebody from HR give us his address.'

'You know they're all about privacy these days. They might want you to get a warrant.'

'Just you leave that with me, Fin, my son. I might be a big, ugly bastard, but I do have my charms.'

'Agreed.'

'With what bit? The ugly bastard or the charm?'

'Let me put it this way, I've never seen you charming.'

'No need to thank me for saving you, cheeky bastard.'

'I think that's us quits now. I don't have the *you owe me one* card to play anymore.'

The medical team took Fiona upstairs to work on her up there.

'The first thing the bastard did was punch her in the face,' Finbar said. 'He knocked her out cold. I want to dance on his fucking bollocks when I get the chance.'

'You and me both, son.' Except Stewart meant he would actually perform a Highland Fling on the man's testicles. He never said he would do something and then failed to carry it out.

Two uniformed officers walked into the PM suite, and Stewart was surprised to see one of them was his driver from the other morning. 'You're like a bad penny,' he said to the young man.

'I am that, sir.'

'What's your name, son?'

'PC Ryan Brick.'

'Prick?'

'Brick, sir. With a *B*.'

'Oh, right. Brick. I thought you were trying to be

a wind-up merchant. Did you get called *Prick* at school?'

'Not twice.'

Stewart grinned. 'I like that. Here's what I want you to do: stick around in here and don't let any bastard in. And I mean, nobody. Under my orders. It's officially a crime scene. Dr O'Toole and Dr Christie got assaulted and slammed into one of those drawers. That's attempted murder. Be on your guard, both of you.'

The second officer didn't look so sure of himself but nodded vigorously, keen to make it through his probation.

'I'm going upstairs with Dr O'Toole to report this,' Stewart said. 'I especially want you to call me if another senior officer should come in here. I'm not expecting him to, but you never know.'

'Superintendent Johnson, sir?' Brick said.

'Aye.' Stewart took out a business card and handed it to the constable. 'Call me if he shows his ugly mug.'

Then he and Finbar left the suite and headed upstairs in the lift. The next level was buzzing with activity, but if anybody knew about the attack downstairs, they weren't letting on.

Duncan Mackay came out of his office again. 'Everything okay with the PM?' he asked O'Toole.

'Oh, everything was fine with his work,' Stewart answered for him, 'but security is a fucking joke.'

Mackay's face fell. Stewart knew the signs from the pub when the big man had one too many whiskies and the fists would start flying, unhindered and unremembered in the morning. It was sobriety that held Mackay back this time, or maybe the fact that the bigger detective would put him on his arse if he lifted a hand to him.

'What do you mean?' Mackay managed to show just enough indignation in his voice, as if Stewart had suggested that Mackay's wife was a secret lap dancer and Stewart had just been to the bank to fill his wallet with singles.

'Somebody attacked Dr O'Toole and Dr Christie in the postmortem suite downstairs.'

'Attacked Finbar? Isn't that usually your angle? Barge into a crime scene and get wired into him with the insults?'

'Get off your bloody high horse. This was attempted murder. Let me talk to the organ grinder.'

'Excuse me?' Mackay took a small step forward, and Stewart had no doubt the pathologist would have taken a swing if he was a) drunk and b) talking to a smaller man. As it was, Stewart would have made sure Mackay could only wipe his arse with a lavvy brush after he'd mastered the art of using it with his teeth.

'You heard. Some bastard jumped them down there, and I want to speak to Patterson about it.'

'*Professor* Patterson has gone for the day. And I need to ask you to show some respect to the man in his own place of work.'

'Oh, aye? How about showing this man some fucking respect?' Stewart said, gesturing to Finbar. 'Treating him like he's some beginner and shoving him downstairs. And putting down an experienced pathologist to help him. You're a real pair of wankers.'

Mackay looked at Finbar. 'You can't talk for yourself now, O'Toole? Not good enough that you try to find the answers to questions that nobody asked. I can't blame the professor for wanting you out of his sight.'

'Is that right? First of all, fuck face, this detective was asking the questions and I can easily ask questions for myself. Cheeky bastard. Maybe if you got your hands dirty more often, we'd have respect for you and that old clown.'

'That's it. Get out and don't come back.'

'Way ahead of you there, chief,' said Finbar. 'You can shove this up your arse. I was prepared to stay for a month, but not now. I'm on sick leave as of now. After being attacked in one of your PM suites. Try to keep money from me and you'll find out who you're really fucking with.'

O'Toole took his doctor's coat off and threw it onto a lab bench before going to the lockers out in the corridor to get his jacket. Stewart followed him.

'That told him,' Stewart said. 'But you won't be able to creep about here like a Peeping Tom looking for clues into the murders of those lassies.'

'You still believe me about them, then?'

'Of course I do. I had to keep an open mind, but after seeing you in that fridge, I think you're dead on. If you'll pardon the pun.' Stewart slapped Finbar on the arm. 'Come on, let's go and find Lisa.'

FOURTEEN

The security room was like a small office with a bank of monitors on one wall. Stewart and Finbar found Lisa sitting beside a chubby man in a black sweater with 'Security' written on the front.

Lisa turned towards the two men as they entered the room. 'I found a holdall in the stairwell. I brought it in here after checking it out. There's a black hoodie in there.'

'Looks like he changed after attacking Dr O'Toole,' Stewart said.

'That's why nothing sticks out on this footage.'

'Do you know what Chris Harris was wearing when he left?' Stewart asked Finbar.

'Just his lab coat, I think.'

'There's no way we can tell if he got dressed in a

black hoodie and came back in to smack you around. Until we talk to him, that is.'

Lisa stood up and patted the security officer on the shoulder. 'Thanks.'

'No problem.'

'I need to find out where this Chris Harris lives,' Stewart said to Lisa, who was picking up the holdall.

The security officer turned to them. 'He lives over in Dennistoun. He had a party there and a few of us went over. It was pretty good.'

'I don't suppose you remember the address?' Stewart said.

'Aye.' The guard wrote it down on a piece of paper and handed it over.

'Thanks, pal.'

They left the office and stood in the corridor.

'Lisa, take that holdall downstairs to the mortuary,' Stewart said. 'There's two uniforms there waiting for forensics. Let them take it. I was going to go round and talk to this Harris guy, but maybe it'll be better if Jimmy Dunbar pays him a visit. Can you make the call? I don't want it to come from me.'

'I'll get right on it,' she replied, and left.

'What are you going to do now?' Finbar asked.

'As soon as we get the black-and-white photos back from Lisa's contact, we can have them printed out and you can show me what you want me to look at.'

'Great. Have them printed out on normal printer paper so I can draw on them.'

'With your crayons?'

'Funny. Let's get a beer,' said Finbar. 'Then I'm going to pack some stuff and move into a hotel.'

'Why?' Stewart asked.

'Because if they're bold enough to try to kill me at work, then trying to do it at my house won't faze them at all.'

'Good point.'

'I need to call my wife.'

'You drive here?' Stewart asked.

'No, I cycled.'

Stewart looked at him.

'What?' Finbar said.

'Nothing. I'll keep my opinion of cyclists to myself.'

'You one of those people who think we shouldn't be sharing the road?'

'I'm one of those people who think fucking cyclists should be joining the Tufty Club so you can learn the fucking Highway Code instead of booting through a red light.'

'That's a privilege that we cyclists have.'

'Bollocks. You know how many times I've nearly had a cyclist as a hood ornament?'

They started walking towards the exit. 'You know we just do it to wind up motorists like you.'

'I bet you do.'

'We do.'

'I should let you cycle home in this pishing rain.'

Finbar laughed. 'I'm not even going to fanny about with my bike. I'll get it later.'

'Fair weather cyclist.'

'I've been called worse.'

FIFTEEN

Senga got off the bus and waited for a wanker in an Audi to get a move on. Posh bastard was deliberately taking his time as if he knew she was desperate for a pee. She could hold it in if she didn't think about it and got a sprint on. The house she was about to clean was just down the road a few houses, not far at all unless your bladder was about to explode like hers was.

The posh sod was on his phone as he drove by, and he didn't even give her a second glance as she stooried across the road, pulling her collar round her neck.

Her husband said she should get a 'wee jalopy', but what he meant was, get yourself a wee scrapper to run about in. They had been retired now for two years, but all dreams of sipping cold drinks on a warm beach had shattered as the price of everything went through the roof. Robbing bastard utility companies were a prime example. So now she had to work a part-time job as a cleaner, just to make ends meet.

Still, she only had two houses to clean today, and this was the second one. The first one was a new place, a single mother and her two teenage boys, who were a right pair of dirty bastards. The oldest one had his own bathroom and didn't even flush after he'd been for number twos. Filthy little bastard. She had told the snooty cow that she would clean the bathrooms, but her sons would do well to look at a YouTube video on how to use the flushing handle on a toilet.

The woman had a high-paying job, if the car and the clothes were anything to go by, but Senga sensed that a man hadn't been in their lives for a long time, and the woman had certainly spared the rod when it came to discipline.

Senga had two boys herself, both grown now, and they would have got a skelp on the arse for not flushing the toilet. There was no excuse for it.

The detached bungalow was painted white with a wee white wall in front. It was very well kept; just what she would have expected from a doctor. He was nice. Very pleasant when he had interviewed her. He said he wanted somebody he could trust. Senga had impeccable references and was given the job on the spot.

Now she had the house in her sights, and it seemed the closer she got to it, the more she needed to pee. Bloody tea. She knew she shouldn't have had that extra cuppa after lunch. 'You know it's a diuretic,' her husband kept saying, as if that was the only big word he knew.

She focused on the white wall, and the wee black gate set into it, holding the key in her pocket, ready to bring it out, slide it into the lock and unbutton her coat as she rushed to the lav.

Then she was there, up the path, key in hand like a tiny medieval battering ram about to take down the portcullis, and she slipped it into the brass lock, turned it and pushed the door open.

She could feel herself starting to dance, one hand unbuttoning her coat while the other pushed the door closed. The dark afternoon had invaded the bungalow like a thick fog. Luckily, she knew where the light switch was without having to look for it.

Her hand reached out, flicked the switch and... Senga didn't have to worry about using the toilet anymore. Would never have to worry about anything again as the darkness turned into a bright light, brighter than anything she had ever seen in her life.

Then it was over.

SIXTEEN

'It's only a matter of time, isn't it?' DS Robbie Evans said, slowing down on Duke Street in Dennistoun.

'What is?'

'Before they bump Stewart out the window. I mean, he's the antithesis of what Police Scotland is all about.'

'And what *is* Police Scotland all about, in your opinion?' Dunbar said.

Evans turned into the one-way street between a bistro and a cash convertor, then jumped on the brakes as a heavy-set man in shorts stepped out in front of the car. He stopped for a moment as if being mowed down was inevitable and started mouthing off.

'I know that fat bastard,' Dunbar said, winding

the window down. 'Chucky Degnan! Move your fucking arse out the way!'

'Not that,' Evans said. 'Or at least the brass aren't looking for that – shouting out the window.'

'Fuck 'em. It's all politics nowadays. You know I'm counting the years until retirement.'

'Not long then.'

'Cheeky bastard. I've got a few to go, son. And I can make your life hell for every single one of those days I have left.'

'Aye, right.'

The big man standing in front of their car squinted his eyes for a moment before recognition kicked in.

'Oh, it's yourself, Mr Dunbar, sir. Have a good yin!' He glowered at Evans before shifting his colossal self across the road.

'Good friend of yours, is he?' Evans said as he put his foot down again.

'We've had our moments. Chucky will toss me a few breadcrumbs now and again, and I'll not knock his bollocks off with my truncheon. He doesn't do anything serious, and if he starts, he knows I'll find out and be all over him like a rash.'

'He's not one of your official confidants, surely?'

'Naw, nothing like that.'

Evans shook his head. 'Why is it always the fat bastards who wear shorts even in freezing weather?'

'It's hardly the Arctic Circle.'

'Aye, but still.' The sky was dark with heavy clouds. The rain had stopped for now, but it was an intermission in the show.

Two streets away was their destination. Evans found a parking space outside the sand-coloured tenement building.

'First floor, Stewart told me,' Dunbar said, looking out his rain-spattered window at the build-ing. Stewart had suggested they take uniforms, but Dunbar didn't see the need just to have a chat.

They got out and walked into the stairway, Evans leading the way.

'Cannon fodder,' Dunbar said to his back as they walked up the stairs.

'Aye, let the young yins do the work. I wouldn't want you putting a hip out.'

'Shut your hole and keep your eyes peeled.'

The stairway was dimly lit and their shoes scuffed the concrete steps. When they got to Chris Harris's landing, Evans stopped short. Dunbar almost bumped into him.

'What's wrong?'

Evans turned to him. 'The front door's ajar.'

'Christ.' Dunbar had had his fair share of walking into a trap before and had learned from the experience. Evans had too, and neither man was ever going to take a chance again.

Dunbar was about to push the door with his shoe when Evans put out an arm. 'I was only joking about you breaking a hip, boss, but let me go in first.'

They drew out their extendable batons.

'Be my guest,' said Dunbar.

Shock and awe. It was the only way to go in. They'd both seen the TV shows where somebody goes into a house and creeps about, making noise and giving a potential attacker a chance to pinpoint where they were. This way, any potential attacker would be taken aback, maybe giving the policemen a precious few seconds to protect themselves.

They each took a room, booting the doors back, and went through the flat like this until they found who they were looking for. No attackers, just Chris Harris, sitting on the settee, blood pouring out of multiple neck wounds, the serrated knife near his hand.

'Check for a pulse, Robbie,' Dunbar said.

'I think he's gone, boss.'

'Do it anyway, son. Just for the report. We tried everything we could except giving mouth-to-mouth.'

Evans carefully stepped round the corpse, while Dunbar automatically kept an eye on the door, in case the killer had followed them in.

'No pulse,' Evans confirmed, looking at his watch.

'As suicides go, it's a messy one.'

'You don't think he killed himself?'

'I've only ever seen this happen once before. Guy stabbed himself in the neck. I'm not saying this isn't suicide, but look at the number of stab wounds.'

'I don't know. Let's keep an open mind,' Evans said, wiping his fingers on the back of his trousers.

'Your Spidey sense should be kicking in by now. We're asked to come and talk to Harris after O'Toole gets shoved into a refrigerated drawer, and we find him dead.'

'Aye, but there's no forced entry.'

'Means fuck all. You see these true crime shows where there's no forced entry and so the detectives assume the victim knew their killer. But how many times have you heard a knock at your door and opened it to some stranger?'

'Never. I'm fucked if I want some Jehovah's Witness trying to come in.'

'Aye, right enough,' Dunbar said. 'They would run circles round you if they got in your hoose. But it could be somebody innocent-looking knocking on doors. Or maybe a bogus gasman. Anybody you wouldn't give a second look at. You open the door, and there's somebody who doesn't look like a threat.'

'Or maybe it really was somebody he knew.'

'Exactly. That's what I'm leaning towards. Harris was expecting somebody. He wasn't working alone.'

'That would make sense. I mean, he's the one who left the mortuary and put the lights out for somebody to come in and give the doctor a belting. Or Harris came back and gave him a belting. What was his motive?'

'Money,' Dunbar said. Then he looked at Harris's left hand. There was a cut on it, a thin slice of red that hadn't been made by the combat knife sitting on the settee beside the rapidly cooling corpse. 'Look at that cut on his left hand.'

Evans looked closer. 'The doc said he sliced the bastard who attacked him. That cut looks slim enough that it could have been caused by a scalpel.'

'I think we have the bloke who attacked O'Toole. Now all we need to find is the person who killed Harris.'

SEVENTEEN

'There's one of your arsehole mates now,' Calvin Stewart said, pointing to a cyclist who had continued cycling through a red light at a pedestrian crossing.

'You're tarring everybody with the same brush,' Finbar complained from the passenger seat.

'No, no, I do realise that there are some very skilled, considerate cyclists. They're called motorists.'

'You're fucking hilarious, Calvin. Just because some baw-heid fires himself in front of a busload of people and the driver has to jump on the brakes and throw those passengers through the window, doesn't mean to say we're all like that.'

'Mark my words, he'll end up under somebody's wheels, scarring the poor bastard for life, all because he doesn't want to wait.' Stewart leaned forward in the seat, peering out the windshield.

'I hope your fucking eyes aren't that bad, honest to God.'

'That's your street ahead and it's blocked off by polis and a fire crew.'

Finbar felt a jolt of electricity run through him as he saw the flashing blue lights of the emergency vehicles blocking the end of his street.

'What the hell's going on?' Finbar said as he saw the smoke rising up in the damp air.

Stewart pulled into the side of the road and a uniform walked over to them. 'Nothing to see here, pal.'

'I see smoke and a lot of fire engines,' Stewart answered.

'Unless you see a circus tent with a bunch of clowns running about, I suggest you move your arse.'

'You're the only fucking clown I can see,' Stewart said, flashing his warrant card.

'Oh, sorry about that, sir.'

'What happened here?'

'A gas explosion levelled a house. They're trying to see if there was anybody inside.'

'What number?' Finbar asked.

'Thirty-one,' the uniform answered.

'Christ, that's my place.'

'Was there anybody in, sir?'

Finbar looked at his watch. 'My housekeeper would have been in there if she was on time. She always comes round later in the afternoon.'

'Let's go and have a look,' Stewart said. 'If it's okay with Acker Bilk.'

Finbar looked puzzled.

'"Send in the Clowns",' Stewart explained.

'I have to say, that makes us look like the fucking clowns.'

'No, it doesn't.'

Arguing about whether Stewart had indeed made an arse of them or not, they walked to Finbar's street. Finbar felt his heart fall into his gut as he saw what was once his home being damped down by the fire service.

'Commander,' Stewart said to the firefighter in charge, showing his warrant card. 'This is my friend's house, Dr O'Toole. He thinks there might have been somebody in the house. His housekeeper.'

The woman nodded. 'We just brought a body out. Deceased. Badly burned.'

'Can you tell if it's a female?'

'Yes, she was burnt but not beyond recognition. We reckon it started with a gas leak in the kitchen.

The walls are thick but not enough to save her. She was found at the front door. She could have switched on a light and a spark could have ignited the gas in the air.'

'Thank you.'

They walked away and Stewart's phone rang. He saw it was Jimmy Dunbar and held up a finger to Finbar as he answered it.

'Jimmy. Did you find that scrote?'

'I did, sir. Very much dead.'

'What? In his flat?'

'Yes. His throat was cut in multiple places. Forensics are here now. The on-call doctor pronounced him dead. It was pretty obvious, but you know how they're sticklers for protocol.'

'Aye, I do that. Any evidence of a fight, or something that we can get prints off?'

'That's the thing. Chris Harris was on the settee, with the knife there. This could go either way. He could, theoretically, have taken his own life.'

'Aye, just like Finbar could have turned on his own gas and blew his own fucking house up.'

'His house blew up?'

'It did. His housekeeper's dead. Jimmy, whoever did this realised that Harris didn't kill Finbar, so they moved quickly to get into his house and cause a gas leak. They want him dead. I don't think Harris killed himself because he fucked up; somebody made it look that way.'

'Christ, that makes it look like somebody at the hospital was involved. How would they have known so quickly?'

'Exactly. Go and talk to him with Lisa. This has to be from you, and not me. Stanley Wank has got it in for me.'

'Don't worry, I'll have a talk with Patterson.'

'Good man. There's nothing more we can do at the doc's house. There's nothing left.'

Stewart hung up. 'Chris Harris has been found dead.'

'Murdered?' Finbar said.

'I think so. They left the knife in his hand, but that doesn't mean he used it on himself. Look at it this way: he tried to kill you, and I don't think he was working alone. He failed, and in the short time since they discovered you weren't dead, they killed him and had somebody turn on the gas to try and kill you. If it wasn't your housekeeper's day to work, that would have been you in the ambulance later on when you came home.'

'Fuck me,' said Finbar. 'They're trying to silence me because I opened my mouth about that young woman. I told them somebody had murdered my niece and the others.'

'Have you got anywhere else to stay?'

'With my sister and her husband.'

'Not a good idea. That's their daughter who was murdered, so they'll know the address. They'll check to see if you're there and you'll be putting them in danger.'

'I could stay at your place.'

'Why don't you fucking shout that a bit louder? I don't think the firefighter with the breathing apparatus on heard you.'

'People would understand.'

'Understand what? That we're now a couple?' Stewart shook his head. 'Besides, I was there in the hospital with you. They could find out where I live. I'm going to pick up some stuff and then we're going to go cap in hand to a friend of mine.'

'What if they're waiting for us when we get to yours?'

'Then they'll get their fucking arse kicked.'

'Do you have gas heating?' Finbar asked.

'Luckily, no. They'll probably use a petrol bomb on me.'

'Yeah, maybe it's best we don't stay at your place. What if they killed us and we were found together?'

'Define *together*.'

'No, I mean, our bodies in the same flat. You do have a second bedroom, don't you? I mean, I'm not averse to sharing or sleeping on the couch, even though my back might not be up to it –'

'Let me fucking stop you right there. There is no way in hell you will ever be sharing a bed with me. I'm going to call my friend and see what he can do for us. If he doesn't have a third bedroom, you can sleep in his dugs' bed. He has a German Shepherd and a Beagle. You can all fight over it.'

They got back in the car. Stewart took out his phone and made a call. 'Jimmy. I need you to do me a solid.'

EIGHTEEN

DCI Jimmy Dunbar was waiting in the car with Robbie Evans when Stewart pulled in with Finbar.

They got out and met on the pavement outside Stewart's building.

'Sorry to hear about your house, Doc,' Dunbar said.

'Thanks, Jimmy. Trying to kill me twice in one day. Makes me think they're going to be relentless.'

'Three young women suffer a heart attack, you start questioning it, and suddenly they want you dead. If somebody's trying to sweep things under the carpet, they're not being very subtle about it.'

'Did you look into the women's backgrounds?' Stewart asked Dunbar.

'I did.'

'Was there anything obvious connecting them?'

'I couldn't find anything connecting them that was obvious. But Robbie here spotted something.'

They all looked at Evans.

'They were all nurses,' Evans told them.

Stewart looked at Finbar. 'Did you know this?'

'I knew my niece was a nurse, but I didn't know that about the other two.'

'Maybe they did have something in common. We're going to have to do more digging,' Dunbar said.

'First things first,' Stewart said, looking up at his flat, 'I should go up there alone.'

'What? Pish,' Finbar said. 'We'll all go up to get your stuff. If one of those tossers is in there, we'll have a wee word.'

'No. I won't put you at risk. You stay down here. I won't have any arguments.'

'We'll go up with you, sir.'

'Fuck the *sir* bit, Jimmy. This is not a normal case we're on.'

'Can we get a move on, Calvin?' Evans said.

'Fucking *sir* to you. Until they boot me out the door with a fake gold watch, I'm still a senior officer.'

'I thought you just said –'

'Unless you changed your name to Jimmy?'

'No, sir.'

'Right. I do appreciate you helping me, though,' said Stewart, 'so don't start greetin' like a wee lassie. I'll get them in tonight in the pub. But let's go. Shock and awe.'

Stewart marched into his stairway and up the first two flights of stairs to his front door.

'I don't know how you manage to get up these stairs when you're pished, Calvin,' Dunbar said.

'Fuck knows. It must be something spiritual. Something in our brains we don't understand. I always make it upstairs, though.'

There was no outward sign that any damage had been done to the door.

'Doesn't mean they didn't pick the lock and wire the handle up to a shotgun,' Dunbar said.

'Are we going to draw straws and see who gets to turn my key in the lock?' Stewart said.

'We drew straws earlier, sir,' Evans replied. 'And you lost.'

'Of course I did.' Stewart took his key out and the other two officers stepped to one side of the door as Stewart put the key in and turned it.

No explosion, no shotgun blast. Nothing. At

least if they went in now and there was somebody waiting for him, they'd have a fighting chance.

The flat was empty. Dunbar took his phone out and turned the torch on, not wanting to tempt fate by switching a light on.

'I know you said you don't have gas,' he said, 'but there's no point in putting it to the test. Maybe one of your neighbours does and *his* gas is filling your flat as we speak.'

'You're full of fucking goodwill cheer, Jimmy.' Stewart looked at Evans. 'Needless to say, don't you go touching anything either.'

'Do I look like my head's zipped up at the back?'

'Don't tempt me.' Stewart turned his attention to Dunbar. 'Will you two check out the rest of the house while I pack some stuff in my bedroom?'

'Nae bother.'

They split up, Stewart heading into his bedroom. He grabbed a holdall from his wardrobe and shoved what clothes he needed into it. He looked around and put some other stuff in, including toiletries. This was a pain in the arse and he promised to sort the bastards who were putting him through this. He had thought it was one person who was doing this, but it was too organised to be just one person. And he knew he would find the answer somewhere in that hospital where Finbar worked.

They had tried to kill the pathologist, and Stewart secretly hoped they would come for him. It had been a while since he had punched somebody in the bollocks.

NINETEEN

Stewart thanked the other two detectives as they all went back downstairs. Finbar had been anxiously waiting and was glad to see them all in one piece.

'Did you check out Manky Malkie Wilson?' Stewart asked Dunbar.

'I did. He's not been in any trouble for a while.'

'Got an address for him?'

Dunbar took out his notebook and rattled off the address for the man who had been the ringleader when Stewart was attacked outside the pub.

'Great. I'm going to have a word with the bastard,' Stewart said.

'Shouldn't you send Lisa instead?' Dunbar asked.

'Nah. This is going to be on the QT. No witnesses. Just me and the doc. That twat has got some answering to do. First of all, Finbar and I are going to go and see a mutual friend of ours. I'm going to ask him a favour.'

'There's one more thing I found out,' said Dunbar.

'What's that?'

'Wilson's a porter at the hospital.'

'The bastard,' Finbar said.

'Keep me in the loop,' Dunbar told Stewart. Then, to Finbar: 'Look after yourself, Doc.'

'I will,' Finbar said, but he didn't look convinced. He'd be looking over his shoulder for a while yet.

Evans and Dunbar left while Stewart and Finbar drove over to a little shop that was the business premises of Michael 'Muckle' McInsh, former detective inspector, now a private investigator.

Inside, a receptionist was at the front desk.

'Well, well, if it isn't big Calvin Stewart himself. Haven't seen you around here in a long time.'

'I couldn't keep away for too long, Maggie, you know that.'

'I knew it! And who is this handsome young fellow?'

'This is Dr Finbar O'Toole.'

'Nice to meet you, Dr Finbar O'Toole.'

'Likewise,' Finbar said.

Maggie turned back to Stewart. 'I'm assuming you haven't come to see me but your friend through the back?'

'As much as I hate to admit it...' said Stewart.

'I'll call through. He usually has a nap at this time of day.'

'I heard that!' Muckle McInsh shouted through from the back office.

'You may as well go through. He has ears like radar.'

'Also heard that!'

Stewart went through the back to McInch's large office. It contained three desks, but only McInch's was occupied. Sparky, his German Shepherd, growled, not recognising Stewart at first; then, before he went into bollock-biting mode, his tail showed signs of recognition.

'Michael, son, how you doing?' Stewart was the only person McInsh knew who called him by his given name.

'Not too bad, Calvin. How's yourself?'

'Shite. Thanks for asking.' Stewart indicated to Finbar behind him. 'Dr Finbar O'Toole, city pathologist.'

'How do?' McInsh said.

'I've had better days,' Finbar replied.

'You said on the phone you needed my help.'

'Aye, we do. See those clothes he's wearing?' Stewart said. 'Those are all his worldly possessions. His house got blown up and he's got fuck all now.'

'What? How the hell did that happen?'

'Somebody's trying to kill him.'

'Really? Can I ask why?'

Sparky walked over to Finbar's outstretched hand and sniffed it, and soon sensed there was no threat.

'His niece and two other young women were murdered, except whoever murdered them made it look like they all had a heart attack.'

'Christ. And now they're after you?'

'They are,' Finbar said. 'This guy shoved me into a refrigerated drawer, and then when that didn't work, they blew my house up. Another pathologist I was working with was also knocked out. She's fine but shaken.'

'Only hours apart, these attacks,' Stewart said. 'They're desperate to get rid of him.'

'How do you know it's more than one person?' McInsh asked.

'Just a feeling,' Stewart answered. 'This seems too sophisticated and when Fin started questioning it at the hospital, there was more than one of them in the room. I might be wrong, of course.'

'Whoever it is, you've got them worried,' said McInsh.

'Exactly,' Stewart said. 'I think they might try and get me too. I've been demoted to desk jockey so I wasn't working a case, but Finbar came to me and told me what was going on so I got involved.'

'Do you need anything from me?'

'Funny you should ask.' Stewart sat down and indicated for Finbar to follow suit. The pathologist sat at one of the other desks.

'Ask away.'

'We need somewhere to stay.'

Both Stewart and Finbar looked at McInsh.

The big ex-DI tapped a pencil on his desk before answering. 'You're in luck. The wife and I are branching out into the flat rental game. We just bought our second place. A wee bungalow. It's still needing done up. An old boy was in it and his family sold it when he passed away. Furniture and all. We haven't cleared it yet, so the furniture is still there. You can stay there for a wee while until we need to start doing it up. Fair enough?'

'Thanks, pal,' Stewart said. 'We'll pay you the going rate. I don't want to take advantage.'

McInsh waved him away. 'You're alright.'

'You and the wife aren't in the charity business. Tell me what you need for it.'

'We'll come up with something if you insist.'

'I do, but I have one question.'

'Shoot.'

'Did the old boy die at home?'

'He did.'

'In bed?'

'Uh-huh.'

'Which bed?'

'It wouldn't be fair if I told you. I would advise putting on some clean sheets, though.'

TWENTY

'I wonder what room he died in?' Finbar said, looking around the bungalow.

'Beggars can't be choosers,' Stewart told him. 'Besides, you're used to death. It's a walk in the park for you.'

'I'm used to cutting up people, not sleeping with a restless spirit.'

'Pish. You don't believe in ghosts and ghoulies, do you?'

'Of course not.'

'You'd better call the wife and tell her what happened.'

'I will,' Finbar said.

He put his bags down in the bedroom he had chosen, hoping to fuck it wasn't the death room.

They had stopped off at Marks and Sparks, where he had bought everything he needed, including new sheets. Stewart had bought some stuff too.

'If I find out any of those bastards in the station are involved in this, they're going to get their hole kicked,' Stewart said.

The house was stale and badly needed to be done up, but it was liveable. Stewart and Finbar had come up with a figure for compensating McInsh. They hoped they wouldn't be here too long.

'Right behind you. I'm going to get wired into Patterson when I see him,' Finbar said.

'Somebody's behind this, though, and not at the hospital. I mean, why would one of the doctors be responsible for the deaths of those girls? Unless he's a serial killer, but I'm not getting that feeling,' Stewart said.

'Go and get those black-and-white photos that you printed at Muckle's office and I'll get the kettle on.'

Finbar walked into the kitchen and found the kettle on the counter. He filled it with fresh water, then took out the teabags and coffee they'd bought at Marks. They would have to get some food in, maybe do a little bit of shopping each day as they needed it.

When Finbar went back into the living room,

Stewart was sitting at a small dining table against one wall with the photos spread out.

'Kettle's on. Go and make us a cuppa while I draw on these photos,' Finbar said. 'I'll show you when you get back.'

Stewart got up and left the living room. 'You don't sleepwalk, do you?' he shouted back to Finbar.

'Give it a rest.'

'It happens. I don't want you dreaming about your wife and next thing you're spooning with me.'

'You should be so fucking lucky.'

Finbar got to work on the photos, and when Stewart came back in with the mugs, he saw Finbar had drawn red pen on the lips of the dead girls. Stewart put the mugs down and sat back in his chair.

'What's this?' he asked, nodding to the photos.

'I first noticed it on my niece when we went to see her in the mortuary,' Finbar said. 'I just happened to notice it, and my friend let me see the photos of the other dead girl. I compared them – and then again, I saw it when I did the postmortem on the third girl. They all had it on their lips.'

'What? Lipstick?'

'Exactly.'

'If you don't mind me saying, this is hardly a fucking breakthrough.'

'Bear with me. Look at where I've coloured the red back in on the photos. It looked to me like the lipstick on each girl had been wiped off and then reapplied, harder in some places.'

Stewart looked closer. 'It looks like you've drawn a letter on each girl's lips.'

'That's exactly what I've done. Look at the first one, letter A. My niece, letter L. The third one, letter D.'

'What the hell does that mean?' Stewart said, sipping his mug of tea.

'ALD. The first three letters in the name Alder.'

'You've lost me.'

'Ten years ago,' said Finbar, 'I testified in the case of a man charged with killing three women near Inverness. His name was Charles Alder. I testified that the women had been killed in the same way. He said he hadn't killed the women, and there wasn't proof, so he was found not proven. Everything was circumstantial. We knew this bastard had killed those women, but we couldn't prove it. He walked out of court a free man.'

Stewart nodded. 'Charles Alder. I'll make a call. See if we can find out where he is.'

'And get this,' Finbar added. 'The three women

who were murdered near Inverness? They were all
nurses.'

TWENTY-ONE

DI Lisa McDonald walked into the quiet incident room and heard a couple of voices coming from Stewart's office. Thinking he and Finbar had come back here, she walked over and gently knocked on the open door. Then saw who was really inside.

Stanley Wang and Doogie Johnson.

'Oh, sorry. I was looking for DSup Stewart.'

'He's not here,' Wang said.

'Right then, I'll be off. Goodnight.'

'Wait. Before you go,' Johnson said, 'I want to ask you how Stewart has seemed to you.'

'Just his normal self,' Lisa answered.

'Then God help us all.'

Wang looked at her. 'He was supposed to be in

here looking over some stats. Did he say where he was going?'

Lisa weighed up her options. She could lie and say she didn't know, but the staff at the hospital might tell Wang and Johnson – or have already told them – that she was with Stewart, and they would wonder why she was lying to them. Or she could go with a bald-faced lie. Option B wouldn't further enhance her career any.

'He asked me to accompany him to the mortuary, sir.'

'Did he say why he was going there?' Wang asked, leaning forward in Stewart's chair.

'Just that he wanted a word with the pathologist there.'

Wang and Johnson exchanged looks.

'Fine,' said Wang. 'But let me give you a piece of advice, DI McDonald: don't get entangled with Stewart. He'll take you down with him.'

'Yes, sir. Will there be anything else?'

'No. Goodnight.'

She grabbed her coat and made her way out, feeling their eyes boring into her.

She would go back to the hospital to check on Fiona Christie. She'd heard the doctor had been kept in for observation. Her nose wasn't broken, but they thought she had banged her head when she hit the floor. At least she'd be safe in the hospital.

TWENTY-TWO

Stewart had just finished inspecting his bed for bugs and any sign of bodily fluids that had been dumped there by a dying man – thankfully, he'd found neither – when his phone rang.

'Lisa. What's up?'

'I want to apologise, sir.'

'Why? What have you done?'

'Dropped you in it, probably.'

'That wouldn't be the first time somebody's dropped me in it.'

'Wang and Johnson were in your office and they asked me where you'd gone. I felt boxed into a corner, sir, and told them where we went. I'm sorry.'

'Don't you apologise, Lisa. Nothing to apologise for. They would have found out and your career would have been at risk. You did the right thing. I can deal with that pair of tossers.'

'*See you tomorrow, sir.*'

'Take care.' Stewart hung up and looked at Finbar. 'Wang and Johnson were snooping about in my office.'

'You trust them?'

'As far as I could spit them. You hungry?'

'Aye, now that I think about it. Why? What you got in mind?'

'I know a wee Thai place that delivers.'

'I like Thai. I was in Thailand once. There's a restaurant there called Phat Phuk,' Finbar said.

'Fat fuck?'

'Aye. But spelled with a *PH*.'

'How do they write *fuck you* over there? With a *PH* as well?'

'No. Phuck U is the manager. This is how he answers the phone: *Phuck U Phat Phuk.*'

'You've been talking to my ex-wife.'

'Seriously. That's how he answers.'

'You're having me fucking on.'

'Phucking On is his brother.'

'Stop talking.'

Finbar laughed. 'Aye, Thai sounds just fine. I could do with some good scran.'

TWENTY-THREE

James Mason had thought about buying a Bentley, something with a bit of class. Not a new one, but something lightly used, where somebody else had taken the hit and the depreciation had kicked in. But his budget would only allow him a car that was years old and that made him feel like a sad bastard who should have been using it for a private hire.

So he had done the next best thing and bought a Lexus. One of his more annoying colleagues had called it a fancy Toyota, but then that same colleague had asked him for a lift one night after his fancy German piece of crap had broken down. Mason had gladly told the man to fuck off.

Glasgow traffic in rush hour was about as much fun as giving yourself a colonoscopy with a garden hose and a magnifying glass, but he was free now, putting his foot down in the big machine. It might just be a hybrid, but this one could pick up its skirts and run like fuck.

The drive to the country estate only took half an hour, but it was like a magic carpet ride, with enough power to overtake the great unwashed. The sky was like a dirty blanket, like the ones at the hospital, all greasy and smelling of piss.

God, he hated that place. It suited him right now, and he was biding his time, but if his plan came to fruition then he would be making a lot more than he made now. The world was his oyster. He hated that saying, but he couldn't think of a better one at that moment.

He felt a jolt of electricity run through him at the thought.

'You okay?' said a voice from the passenger seat.

He jumped slightly, keeping his eyes on the road but tightening his hands on the wheel. He had completely forgotten she was there. Usually, they were all chatty and excited, but this one was more... relaxed. Carla White was a fair bit older than the others, had been round the block a few times, but she was more than up for it. He hated to use the word *groom*, because that made him feel like a paedo, but

that was what it was. Give them the spiel, promise
them the earth, bring them here, and Bob's your aunt
Fanny.

'I'm fine. Why?' he replied, smiling. It was an
act. He should have been on the stage, he was such a
good actor. He'd missed his calling. Bringing back
people from the brink of death was okay, of course,
but having people fawn over your every move was far
superior.

Just like Sunshine, the man they were going to
see now, spend the whole weekend with. Never
mind that a whole gaggle of other guests would be
there. He, the mighty James Mason, was the important one. He was the gift giver. That's what Sunshine
had called him. The gift giver. James Mason practically walked on fucking water. He was unstoppable.
Especially when he had his gifts with him.

'You looked like you were miles away.'

He looked over to Carla and smiled. His big,
wide, boyish-charm smile. Although the fire behind
his eyes was going full tilt, he kept it hidden. 'Just
thinking about the fun we're going to be having this
weekend.'

She laughed. 'I've been looking forward to this.'

I bet you fucking have. No cold beans out of a tin

for you this weekend. Only the finest champagne and caviar and as much fun as you can handle.

'Me too.'

It was Carla's first time coming with him and he knew she was going to fit right in. The little pack of needles he had in his travelling case would see to that.

If he played his cards right, Glasgow would be a distant memory by next week.

TWENTY-FOUR

DI Lisa McDonald sat at her dining table while Alice, her six-year-old daughter, sat on the couch playing with her dolls. Lisa didn't date these days. She had been on plenty of dates in the past, and then when they found out she had a daughter with Down's Syndrome, they didn't call back. Add in to the mix that she had her younger brother, who had learning disabilities, living with her, and that was it over. Add into the mix that her grandfather – a cranky old Irishman called Liam – also lived with her, and that was the final nail in the coffin.

Bella, the little lemon Beagle, barked at something she heard outside and jumped onto the back of the settee in front of the window, shouting at a dog three floors below.

Lisa looked at the dog. No, Bella was the final nail. Her sweet little rescue dog who was her protector now.

'Bella, for feck's sake, will ye give it a rest!' Liam said. 'Lisa, I don't know how your brother can play those video games with all this racket. Even with headphones on.'

Alice laughed at the dog as her tail wagged furiously.

'He's used to it, Grandad,' said Lisa.

'And how you can concentrate on what you're doing is beyond me. How does the bloody dog know when there's another mutt outside?'

'Sixth sense. Just like she knows to run away when you take your socks off.'

'Oh, here, that's below the belt. My feet never stink, they just omit an odour that recreates a summer meadow.'

'Your feet stink, Grandad,' Alice said. She always called him Grandad too.

'Aye, ye're right, darlin'. There's no fooling you.'

Bella finished her shouting out the window, jumped back down and curled up beside Alice on the floor.

'What is it you're looking at?' Liam asked Lisa.

She looked across at him. 'Photos of...some friends of a friend.'

Liam gave a little nod. He understood that it was work related. 'Can I have a look?'

'Aye, no problem.'

The old man got up from the settee and came over to the dining table and sat down. Three black-and-white photos were laid out and she had drawn red on the lips, following the directions Finbar had given her over FaceTime. He'd guided her and shown her his copies.

'The red pen on the photo is where the lipstick was thicker on the women when they were found. Like each one was a letter. A-L-D.'

'What's that supposed to mean when it's at home?' asked Liam.

'Finbar testified against a killer ten years ago. Charles Alder. He was found not proven in the deaths of three women.'

'And this Finbar thinks that Alder's up to his old tricks again?'

'It's a possibility.'

'Why doesn't your boss look into it then?'

Lisa looked at Liam. 'This is just speculation. We can see this because we're colouring it in, but this would never hold up in court. We'd be laughed at.

Finbar thinks this is a subtle dig at him. And the second victim, Ashley Smith, was his niece. If it is Alder, then he made it personal.'

'How did he kill them?'

'That's the thing: they each died of a heart attack. Their deaths were listed as natural causes. Not murder.'

'He's a clever sod, eh? If it is indeed murder, then he's getting away with it. Taunting Finbar by murdering his niece.'

'They tried to kill Finbar twice today.'

'What?' Liam shouted, and Bella looked over to see if she could sink her teeth into somebody who was bothering her master, but just put her head back down. Her Duckie soft toy would be getting a real going-over later, but for now, the duck would live.

'He got attacked in the mortuary and shoved into one of the drawers. Then his housekeeper was killed when his house blew up. Fire service think it was a gas leak and the poor woman flicked on a light switch and set it off.'

'God Almighty.'

'The thing is, I'm thinking that this Alder guy was taunting him, but now that Finbar is suspicious about the deaths, he's taken it to a whole new level.'

'How are that pair at the station reacting to it?'

'Wang and Johnson? They're not interested.'

'Figures. You've been saying they're a pair of... idiots for a long time now.' He looked over at Alice, who hadn't batted an eyelid.

'They're about as useful as a chocolate fireguard.'

'So, what are you going to do now?'

'I think it's best if we look more closely at the dead girls' backgrounds. I called Jimmy Dunbar earlier. He was talking to Calvin Stewart. They're going to talk to the families.'

'It's one thing having suspicions but another finding proof.'

'I know,' said Lisa. 'But the way they're going after Finbar, I think they're going to show their hand sooner rather than later.'

Liam frowned. 'As long as they don't kill Finbar in the process.'

TWENTY-FIVE

'I hope this Thai doesn't come back on me,' Stewart said, burping out the window of the car.

'Fuck me. As chat-up lines go, I've heard better.'

'Trust me, son, I get my fair share. I know when to rein it in. I can be as charming as the rest.' He looked at Finbar. 'Got any mints?'

'I don't need them, chief. When I'm talking to a woman, I tend to control my bodily functions and not blow their wig off with rifting.'

'Whatever. But you'll be smelling like fried rice for the rest of the night.'

'Sake. Here.' Finbar reached into his pocket and pulled out a packet of gum and handed a piece over.

'What's that pish?'

'It's mint flavour.'

'Aye, but it's no' a fucking mint, is it? I never asked for chewing gum. Christ, I'd blow a bubble and have the bastard wax my fucking eyebrows or something.'

'Suit yourself.' Finbar popped a piece into his mouth as Stewart turned his attention to the tenement they were watching.

Cars swished past on the wet roads, their headlight beams dancing across the rain-splattered windscreen. It had dried up now, but it looked like there might be snow later.

'You sure this is the right address?' Finbar asked, playing with the front passenger window, making it go up and down.

'It is. And will you stop playing with that fucking window? You're like a five-year-old.'

Finbar tutted and kept the window up. 'I'm bored. I don't know how you suits and boots do this all day. I'd be taking a machine gun to some bastard just before I went out in a blaze of glory.'

'You've been watching too many action films. Blaze of glory indeed. This is why I carry a warrant card and you shove your hands inside dead people for a living.'

'You just shove your hand inside a living person.'

'Haven't done it yet, son, but there's a first time

for everything.' Stewart gave Finbar a sideways look. Then he looked across the street and turned the engine off. 'There's the bastard now.'

Finbar had grabbed the door handle, but Stewart put a hand on his arm. 'Easy. We don't want to spook him.' He took his hand off. 'I'm going to ask you again: you sure you want in on this?'

'Of course I do. Ashley meant the world to me, and if that Wilson arsehole had anything to do with her death, I want to look him in the eyes.'

'Fair enough. Let's go.'

They got out, the orange sodium lights shining on the wet road. The place was dank and foggy.

They approached the stairway door and saw it didn't have any electronic measure to keep somebody out. Stewart turned the handle and pushed the door open.

They heard a door close upstairs and made their way up quietly. Stewart knocked on the door.

'Fuck's sake, you're early,' Manky Malkie Wilson said, yanking the door open.

'I think we're just in time, don't you?' Stewart said, pushing his way in. Wilson's eyes went wide, stretching the cut on his forehead where Stewart had headbutted him.

'You cannae dae this! Get the fuck oot!'

'Hear that?' Stewart said. 'He just invited us in for a wee chat.'

Finbar grinned and shut the door behind him.

'I'll have you arrested for this!' Wilson said.

'Arrested for what? Inviting us in for a wee cup o' tea?' Stewart looked at Wilson, who didn't seem so brave now that the detective was sober. 'Maybe I'll make a pre-emptive strike and have some of my men come round and arrest you for assaulting a police officer.'

'You stuck it on me first!'

Stewart pushed the man into the living room. 'Sit down, bawbag. And I was outnumbered four-to-one. Who do you think a jury's going to believe, a convict like you or a decorated officer like me? Especially when I have other witnesses. I'll make sure the word gets spread around inside that you were very cooperative with us polis. You'll have an arsehole bigger than a sausage roll by the time they're finished making you Valentine's cards.'

Wilson sat on a chair. 'That's shite.'

'Is it, Malkie? No, let me tell you what was shite: you and three of your fucking chav mates jumping me the other night. You were there for Finbar, but saw the opportunity to give me a belting first. Tell me if I'm wrong.'

Wilson said nothing.

'Thought so,' Stewart said, carrying on. 'So what was it? You lot failed so they got to Harris, got him to finish the job? We know you work in the hospital as a porter. Friends with Harris were you?'

'So what? I'm friends with a lot of people there.'

'But don't worry, we know Chris Harris attacked the good doctor here in the hospital, but I'll damn well make sure forensics find your prints in the mortuary too.'

'As you just said, I'm a porter in the hospital. My fingerprints are all over the place.'

'That's fine then. They'll find them in the lower-level mortuary too. A place that normally lies empty. No need for you to be down there. They'll find them on the drawer the doctor was shoved into. In the office where he and another pathologist were attacked. Your prints and your pal Harris's.' It was a bluff and they both knew it but sometimes getting them riled up worked.

Wilson started sweating. 'Look, I didn't attack anybody down there. I had nothing to do with that, and I haven't heard anything about anybody getting attacked. I don't know Chris Harris to talk to. If he did attack the doctor, then that was on him.'

'No, not on him,' Finbar said. 'He didn't just

decide to let me have it. It was well planned. Just like you and your cronies coming to the pub to give me a kicking.'

Wilson shook his head. 'Look, I had nothing to do with you being attacked in the mortuary.'

'But you were going to attack him outside the pub,' Stewart said, not phrasing it as a question.

'We were paid to put the frighteners on him, that's all. We weren't going to give it to him hard. Just a wee bit of fisticuffs.'

'Fisti-fucking-cuffs? You think this is a fucking joke? My bastard leg is giving me gyp, ya wee bastard.' Stewart stepped forward and stood on Wilson's bollocks before the man could move. Wilson let out a squeal and Stewart backed off.

'That's your starter for ten. You tell me who wanted Dr O'Toole out of the picture or what I just did will feel like eating a sponge cake.'

'I don't know who he is,' Wilson said. 'I haven't seen him around the hospital, but he was waiting in the car park when I left one day. Said he knew who I was and maybe word would get around what sort of guy I was and they would kick my arse to the kerb if they found out.'

'Who's *they*?'

'The management. HR. Whoever. He said there

could be an easier way to deal with this. He gave me an envelope with money. Told me to recruit a few friends and go visit the doctor at the pub. Find out what night he would be in the local where he drinks after work sometimes. There was a couple of grand in there. I gave the boys a few hundred each and told them all we had to do was give him a fright.'

'You knew where to find me,' Finbar said.

'I just asked around. It was easy. You're a very popular bloke, Doctor. By the way, there's a wee nurse on level –'

'I'm a married man,' Finbar said.

Wilson shrugged. 'Well, she likes you. I'm just sayin'.'

'Well, stop fucking sayin',' Stewart said. 'You think you can use psychology on us by talking about something else. I'm used to talking with wee dildos like you in an interview room.'

'That's why you're round here bothering me now?' Wilson shot back. 'Why don't you have me in the station? Naw, that wouldn't be too clever, would it? What would your boss say about that? I don't think he'd be too happy if he knew you were round here.'

'What do you know about my boss?' Stewart said.

'Nothing.'

'Again with the psychology,' Finbar said to Wilson. 'He doesn't give a fuck if his boss knows.'

'That right?' Wilson said.

Stewart laughed. 'Aye, that *is* fuckin' right. Nobody knows we're here. In fact, I could throw you over the banister on your landing and we'd be off like fucking ghosts. You have no proof.'

Stewart made a sudden move that caused Wilson to screech, and he grabbed Wilson's phone out of his pocket. 'I'll dump it in a bin outside. Just in case you thought about filming us when we left.' He put it into his pocket.

Wilson made a face that suggested that was exactly what he had been thinking.

'Right, the names of those other fucks you were with when you jumped me.' Stewart thought that Wilson was going to give him a hard time, earning him another step onto his bollocks, but Wilson didn't believe in honour among thieves.

'Bruce Latimer, Colin Coffin and Peter Boyle.'

'Colin Coffin? That Joe Coffin's laddie?' Stewart asked.

'Aye.'

'His fucking old man's a wee dick. Like father, like son, I can see. But let me tell you what's going to happen now, Malkie. You're going to tell me the name of the bloke who gave you the envelope, or I'm going to talk to your pals and tell them you shafted them big style.'

'How can I tell you his name when I don't know it?'

'Does he work in the hospital?' Finbar asked.

'I've seen him around before, but he's no' a porter like me.'

'We didn't think he was a fucking porter,' Stewart said. 'Where have you seen him?'

'Just in passing. I think he's a doctor.'

Stewart and Finbar exchanged looks.

'I know you young bastards live on your phone. You do everything on it, from playing games to downloading porno,' Stewart said. 'So tell me I'm wrong when I suggest you took a photo of him.'

'Oh God,' Wilson said. 'Please don't.'

Stewart took the phone out of his pocket. 'I'm going to keep this for a while with your permission. Do I have your permission to keep this and look through it until I can get it back to you?'

'Naw. I give you fuck all.'

'Interesting. Dr O'Toole will be my witness that I found this phone out on the street. Somebody must have dropped it. And what do you know? It was unlocked. Now give me your code to unlock it.'

'Nope.'

'Listen, son, I'm going to get that code even if I have to shove your filthy skids down your throat until you gag it out. And if I have to break a sweat doing this, then when I do get it open and identify the man who gave you the money, I'll be sure to tell him your name. I'll even spell it for him. I'll tell him you couldn't wait to drop him in it. Man like that? I reckon he has a lot of friends who can do work for him even if he's incarcerated. What say you, Dr O'Toole?'

'Well, after giving it some serious consideration, I reckon you're right. Man with that power and money? Malkie here will be lucky if he lasts the weekend inside. They'll find him hanging by a towel in the showers.'

'Or maybe his knob will be cut off with a sharpened toothbrush. Self-inflicted, of course.'

'Come on, Mr Stewart,' Wilson said. 'This isn't funny.'

'Do you see us laughing? I'll drop you down the fucking shitter quicker than a rabid badger. You'll be totally fucked. Or...you can give me the code, and give me permission in front of a witness to rummage through your phone.' Stewart held out the phone in front of Wilson's face. 'If you grab this, I'll wrap my boot so far round your nut sack, you'll be able to audition for the Scottish Ballet. And not as a man, in case you didn't get the reference.'

'Sake. You think I want your size twelves on my manhood again? The code is twelve, zero-three, ninety-seven.'

Stewart took the phone away and tapped in the code, and the phone screen popped into life. 'Nice. But I could have guessed that I suppose: your mental age, your knob size and your IQ.'

'Funny.'

'Do you see me laughing?' Stewart asked, not looking at the younger man but poking a finger at the photo app. There was the usual detritus that lived in a photo app, but then Stewart saw photos of a dour day in the hospital car park. A bus shelter to be more specific.

A man in a dark coat was walking towards the shelter. The glass was dirty and streaked with the remnants of a morning shower, but the man's face could be seen clearly.

'You recognise him?' Stewart asked, showing Finbar the photo.

Finbar looked at it. Shook his head. 'No. But

there are so many doctors there that it would be impossible to know every one.'

'What did he sound like?' Stewart asked Wilson.

Wilson shrugged. 'Scottish. But more like a posh twat. Not an upper-class English guy, but a Scots guy who was trying too hard.'

Then the penny dropped. 'James Mason,' Finbar said. 'I saw the twat in the canteen one day, being all hoity-toity and degrading one of the canteen workers. If I'd been next to him in line, I'd have told him to piss off, but nobody said a word to him. I remember thinking what an arrogant prick he was.'

'So this guy Mason is a doctor,' Stewart said to Wilson, 'and he gave you money to beat the crap out of the doctor here. And you took it.'

'I told you, I didn't have a choice.'

'Everybody has a choice, son.' Stewart said. 'Did he give you a number to call or text when the job was done?'

'Text. Under "The Umbrella Man".'

'Thanks for letting me look at your phone. I'll make sure you get it back soon. But if you decide you're going to text Mason, telling him that I was here, just remember one thing: women have died, and if he's responsible, then he will have no hesitation in killing you. He'll just make it look like a heart attack.'

Wilson stood up. 'Fuck this. I'm going to live with my auntie for a while. That mad bastard won't find me.'

'You do that, son. And when you come back, make better decisions. If I ever find out you've been near the good doctor here again, I'll have somebody rip your fucking nuts off. Do we understand each other? No arrests, no going to court, but you'll have changed sex overnight.'

'Crystal clear.' Wilson looked at Finbar. 'I'm sorry. I needed the money. We weren't going to put you in hospital, just scare you a bit. Turns out, you scared the shit out of me when you put a scalpel down my trousers.'

'That's nothing to what that fucking doctor's going to get,' Finbar said.

Stewart and Finbar left and got into the car.

'Fin, you do understand that none of this would hold up in court?'

'I do.'

'That's why I threatened him. What we did was illegal – me taking his phone, threatening him with violence. He had to know what will happen to him.'

'Things are moving fast,' Finbar said. 'Somebody

wants me out of the picture for questioning the deaths of the young women and it looks like they'll stop at nothing.'

'We need to find this prick of a doctor. I can have a friend of mine find out where he lives.'

Finbar shook his head. 'Mason's only the tip of the iceberg. If he's responsible for the deaths, we can nail him. But I think it goes much further than him.'

TWENTY-SIX

There was a tall man standing at the gatehouse. Mason had seen him before on previous trips. He was ex-army or some such nonsense. All baldy and muscles that could rip your arms off if he had a notion to.

The bright lights caught the man's hi-vis vest and Mason kept the full beams on just to annoy him. The guard put a hand up in front of his eyes as Mason rolled to a halt.

Baldy glared at him as he rolled his window down, not speaking for a few seconds but looking intensely at him. 'Name,' he said.

Mason had lined up a few shots to fire at the gorilla, but he didn't waste his breath.

'James Mason.'

'Like the actor?'

'Like the doctor.'

The same fucking dance every time. Same question, same response, same little laugh to himself as he checked his clipboard. Mason pictured ramming the pen into the ex-soldier's eyeball.

'Right. You're on the list. Drive up all the way and turn –'

Mason floored the accelerator. He wasn't listening to any more drivel. He'd been here many times and getting directions was just having the piss taken out of him.

'Nice place,' Carla said as the lights cut through the darkness and they opened out into the approach to the big house, which itself was lit up like a Christmas tree.

'It is.' He wished it was his. He felt a twinge of envy course through him. The man who owned this had money dripping out of his arse. It wasn't fair. Money threw itself at him. He didn't have to work hard for it; not like Mason, who had to save actual lives to get a salary.

This man made fuckers laugh. That was it. Entertained people. And see what his spoils were: a huge house, any car he wanted and any woman he wanted.

'I wish I lived in a place like this,' Carla said.

Mason screamed in his head, *Shut up, bitch!*

The car pulled up into the courtyard, where a butler was waiting. It was the old one again this time, the pain in the arse with a twang that a fucking sheepdog wouldn't understand.

Mason opened his own door as the kilted figure opened the passenger door for Carla. He heard what could only be described as a language spoken by a person mid-stroke.

Two younger men came across when the boot was popped, one prepared to get behind the wheel, the other ready to get the luggage. Mason was disappointed to see one of them had the clichéd red hair.

'Mr Mason, sir, gid tae see ye again,' the old butler said, and Mason interpreted it as some Highland greeting his ancestors used to scream before they ran down a hill into cannon fire.

'Nice night,' was all he managed to reply.

'Ach, it's braw.'

Something about haggis for supper, or something. Mason skipped round the car after handing the miscreant his car keys, with a glare and a warning to 'keep it out of a fucking ditch', and guided Carla by the elbow before she made an attempt to engage the man in conversation.

The old boy followed them into the reception area, where there was a huge fireplace with a roaring log fire keeping the cold at bay.

'It's just like a real castle,' Carla said.

It is *a real fucking castle,* Mason thought, but he merely smiled. He turned to see the young lad with the cases come in and drop them on the stone floor.

'Easy, son,' Mason said, looking at the smaller case with the goods in it.

'Tak it awa',' the old boy said, showing off his expert knowledge of Klingon.

Mason grabbed the small case as the useless inbred grabbed the bigger cases. A young female sat behind a desk in the lobby, as if this place was a real hotel, and told the boy which room to take the cases to.

Then a voice boomed out at Mason. 'James! You made it!'

Sunshine himself came strolling out of the room on the right, holding a crystal glass full of the best amber fluid money could buy.

'Sunshine! Good to see you!'

'And who is this young filly?' Sunshine asked, his eyes taking in the sight in front of him.

'Sunshine, this is Carla White. Carla, Mr Sunshine.'

'Pleased to meet you,' Carla said, holding out a hand.

Sunshine shook it. 'Welcome to my Scottish hideaway. Have fun.'

'I'll try.'

'Mason, if I may steal you away for a minute? Carla, one of my men will get you a drink through in that ballroom.'

'Thank you,' she said, and walked away.

'This is the goods?' Sunshine said, taking Mason by the elbow and leading him through another doorway, into a private lounge that was empty.

'It is.' Mason smiled as the door was closed behind him, and then, suddenly, Sunshine's demeanour did a one-eighty.

'I have to say, this is not up to the usual standard, James. I am disappointed.'

Mason's jaw dropped. 'It's the real deal. Just like always. High-grade stuff.'

'I'm not talking about the stuff,' Sunshine said, and once again Mason heard the man's rough East End upbringing coming to the fore, pushing aside the cultivated posh accent. 'I'm talking about what you Scotch people call a fucking old boiler.'

Fuck. He meant Carla.

'She's only just turned thirty,' said Mason.

'Thirty, my old son? Thirty is practically pension age.'

'She's been on my radar for a while.'

'Those other three were in their twenties. That's perfect. They're young, and fun. Just enough experience to enjoy a good time and still have their looks about them. This thing? Fuck me, squire, her skin looks like orange peel.'

'She can get the stuff you want.'

'So can other women. Take her home. Don't unpack your bags. Come back some other weekend when you've got a decent-looking tart on your arm. Where did those other girls go? Scare them off with your personality? I have to say, I am not a happy camper.'

Mason couldn't help but show his disappointment. 'Look, Sunshine, I've done everything you asked of me. I brought my A game to this show. I've supplied some good gear and brought you the girls who were not only eye candy but who supplied some of the stuff. All that takes time and effort, you know that.'

'I do know that. Don't make it sound like I was drugging those girls and having my way with them. I enjoyed their company, that's all.'

'Enjoyed having the gear they brought. Fuck me, we all took a huge risk.'

'Me included.'

'I know, Sunshine. I'm not saying you didn't, but you're better protected than any of us.'

'I enjoyed my time in your company, James, but sometimes good things must come to an end. I think we should conclude this partnership.'

'How will you get your stuff?'

Sunshine smiled, but there was zero humour in it. He put a hand on Mason's arm. 'Don't worry about it. Look, why don't we have a good time now that you're here, and in the morning you can leave quietly. I'll have somebody drop Carla off.'

'So this is it? The end of our arrangement?'

'I'm afraid so. It has to be this way.'

Mason nodded slowly. 'If that's the final decision, then so be it. I'd like to enjoy your hospitality one more time, then I'll be out of your hair tomorrow.'

'No problem. There are some people here that you know. Have a good time, James.'

Sunshine smiled and left the room, leaving James to stand in front of the log fire that was blazing in the fireplace. He knew this was a room that an amorous couple could occupy with complete privacy.

He turned and walked out, closing the door behind him. He went into the ballroom, where Carla was standing talking to an older bloke, a champagne flute in her hand. He approached her and gently grabbed her by the elbow.

'Please excuse us,' he said to the old coffin-dodger.

'Absolutely, old chap,' the old boy said, and turned away to another young woman.

'What's wrong?'

'Old Sunshine doesn't want us here.' Mason looked around to make sure they weren't being overheard.

'What? You said this would be alright. You promised me. Fun and games, you said. A pathway to a better life.'

'And it will be. He's not all there, that's all.'

'You mean he's a secret nut job? Well, that's just magic.'

'No, nothing like that,' said Mason. 'I mean, he's got so much money that he's not in touch with reality, that's all. You saw the old teuchter who helped us out of the car. Sunshine gets off on that shite. Look at me, I'm the big bloke because I can afford Harry Lauder to greet my guests as they arrive at my country pile. He makes his money too easily.'

'The public love him.'

'I know they do. Bloody fools. If they only knew. Oh, and he thinks you have skin like orange peel.'

'Cheeky bastard.'

'I know,' Mason said. 'Like he's a fucking oil painting.'

'You've done a lot for him, went above and beyond. All the promises he made, and now he's cutting you loose. Bastard.'

Mason smiled. 'He doesn't know who he's fucking with.'

'He used you. He knew what he was doing and he got you to cover. Now he's cleaning house.'

'Don't worry. I always had a contingency plan.'

'Do tell.'

'Not here. Later, in my room.'

Carla looked around at the other guests. 'So what do we do now?'

'We have a good time. Drink and be merry. Then, tomorrow, we leave.'

Mason looked over at Sunshine, who was now having a drink with a young woman. May he rest in peace.

TWENTY-SEVEN

'No arrests, no warrants. Now I'm getting to see the other side of policing,' Finbar said as they drove away from Malkie Wilson's flat.

'Aye, well, sometimes we have to skirt around the law. They give us what we want and we don't throw their arse in prison. It's a system that worked a long time ago, and it's frowned upon now, but needs must. If we want to get who killed your niece, this is the time to take shortcuts. Agreed?'

'Too right. We live in a world where the scum get a slap on the wrist while some poor bastard is too scared to go out again. I'd hang the bastards.'

Stewart had checked his phone and a text was waiting for him with James Mason's address. They drove along to Bearsden, where the address was.

'I'm surprised you don't live here,' Stewart said.

'My house was in a nice area, wasn't it?'

'Not saying it wasn't, but this is where money goes to live.'

'I'm not a millionaire.'

'Neither is this Mason joker,' Stewart said, turning into a street with a garden on the corner that would have been called the local five-a-side pitch in a poorer part of the city.

It was a well-lit street, with big houses on either side. Mason's was halfway up, with a U-shaped driveway in front. Stewart stopped the car on the street and got out, then poked his head back in.

'If he *is* in, don't make eye contact with the bastard,' he told Finbar.

'Eye contact? He's a surgeon. He'll be operating on his own arsehole when I'm done with him.'

'Meantime, keep a low profile.'

Stewart shut the door and walked up the driveway to the front door. There were no lights on inside. The curtains were drawn, which meant Mason didn't want anybody looking in if he was out somewhere. Stewart looked at his watch; the doctor could be out having dinner or something. He rang the bell anyway.

No answer.

After a few minutes, he turned and walked back to the car and got in. 'Nobody's in. Never mind, I'll have Jimmy Dunbar come and talk to him over the weekend.'

'Maybe it's just as well he's not in.'

'Right, Fin. Let's go and see your sister.'

Sunshine lay on the bed, the needle by his side. 'Tell James to come and see me,' he said to his assistant. 'Then you're off duty for the rest of the night.'

The man scuttled away and Sunshine was now floating in the air, mentally. He'd been plagued by a back injury for years which had robbed him of a good night's sleep. Painkillers hadn't worked. Narcotics hadn't worked. Then he met Dr James Mason through a friend of a friend and the man had been the answer to his prayers. He had been about to retire from television when Mason had suggested a little cocktail of liquid meds, and then he was hooked.

His new TV show was an instant hit. *Mr Sunshine.* It was now his nickname to all his friends too. But coming up to Scotland for the weekend was his weakness. It was ironic that he could afford this place now and yet he was going to have to spend more time in London. He needed friends down there and not just the fair weather kind either. He had thought that James was in the fold, but now he wasn't sure. That was why he had told the man to go home.

The assistant was back, appearing like a fucking ghost again. The man was competent, but by God, he moved about like he was levitating rather than walking. More than once Sunshine had nearly shat himself after his assistant had appeared as if by magic, creeping about behind him.

'Mr Mason for you, sir.'

Sunshine snapped his eyes open. 'What have I told you before? Make a fucking noise when you come into the room. Rattle the door knob, or cough, or do some fucking thing. Instead of trying to give me a heart attack.'

'Yes, sir.' The man bowed and left the room.

'Creepy bastard. His arse is toast. When I leave for London, I'm fucked if I'm taking him with me.'

'The London thing is still on, then?' Mason said, sitting in a chair. Next to it was a side table with a bottle of champagne and two glasses. One had been used.

'Yes. I'm sorry I spoke to you that way earlier,

getting ratty about that bint you brought tonight. My head wasn't in a good place. But yes, I'm going ahead with the plans, and I wanted to say that I want you on board. I want you to get me that stuff you make up.'

Mason looked at the man, at the champagne and at the vial on the table next to the bottle.

'Wait. You didn't take any of the stuff I gave you, did you?'

Sunshine looked over at him. 'Yes. Why? It's as good as it ever was. Like the rest of the stuff you brought me.'

Except this isn't the same stuff, daft bastard.

Mason suddenly stood up. Sunshine wanted him after all, to go to London, where he would rub shoulders with famous people, make the kind of money he'd only ever dreamed of. Sunshine had promised him. Mason would live a life of luxury as Sunshine's personal doctor. He would be able to give the man stuff to sleep, stuff to wake up and everything in between. Mason would be the key to keeping the man on his toes, able to work, to make millions. They would look after each other.

'You should have told me earlier you were planning on keeping me around, Sunshine.'

'I'm sorry, James. I felt insulted that you would

bring that older woman to my house. Her face is familiar, though. I can't place it.'

'She's a brilliant chemist. She and I were working on something that's even better than what I've been giving you. Something that would make you sleep and wake up feeling not only fantastic but pain-free.'

'Oh. You should have told me. Is that what she does for a living? Pharmacist?'

'Not exactly. She's just good at playing around with drugs. How much of the cocktail did you take?'

'All of it. Just like always.'

'Shite.'

'What's wrong?' Sunshine asked, suddenly sitting up.

'Stay still. You don't want to raise your blood pressure,' Mason said, walking towards the bed, feeling panic rise up inside him. 'Why didn't you tell me you were going to take me to London? You stupid, stubborn man.'

'Here, that's not very nice. I can always change my mind, you know.'

'Too late for that, I'm afraid.'

'Is it?' Sunshine sneered at Mason.

'Yes. You're going to have a heart attack in about ten seconds.'

TWENTY-EIGHT

Ken Smith and his wife, Mary, were still raw after their daughter's death.

'Hello, sis,' Finbar said as they went into the house. 'This is my friend Calvin Stewart.'

'Pleased to meet you,' Mary said, leading them through to the living room.

Ken Smith was a tall, skinny man. He shook Stewart's hand, but the handshake was limp and weak as if his hand was made of wet paper.

'You boys like a drink?' he asked, a brief smile flitting across his face. He had been hitting the bottle hard and he seemed pleased at the prospect of having two new drinking buddies.

'Not now, Ken, thanks,' Finbar said, sitting down

on the settee beside Stewart, who had already taken a load off. 'Maybe a cup of tea.'

'Tea. Aye.' Ken's face fell at the idea, but he scuttled out of the room.

'How are you holding up?' Finbar asked his sister.

Mary sat on a chair with the remote control on the arm. She used it to mute the show.

'I still can't believe it, Fin. My wee girl. Gone.'

'I can't either. But I'm glad to say that DSup Stewart here believes us.'

Mary looked up sharply at Stewart. 'You do?'

Stewart nodded. 'I do. We have another victim who died in exactly the same way as your daughter and the other girl. Twenty-something girls don't just die of a heart attack. I think they were given something undetectable that killed them.'

'Somebody murdered my Ashley?' She said it as if she was only now realising it after being given a professional opinion.

'I would say so. And somebody wants to stop us from going any further with this investigation. They tried to kill your brother twice. He's getting close and they want to stop him.'

'Oh, Fin, no. You need to stop. I can't lose you too.'

'We're not giving up now, Mary. We think we know one of the people who's involved.' Finbar looked at her. 'Did Ashley ever mention a surgeon by the name of James Mason?'

'James? Yes. She mentioned him a few times. He's a brilliant surgeon, she said. All the girls know him. He's a bit of a ladies' man. She liked him a lot. Not as boyfriend material, obviously, but he has a lot of friends.'

'So she socialised with him?' Stewart said.

'Not in that sense. She and some others went to a party thrown by one of his friends. Ken and I weren't happy about it and told her to be careful, but she came home in one piece. She said she'd had a good time. Then another time she said she was going to a party again, but this time her friends weren't going. She told me not to worry the night she left for the party. We never saw her alive again.' Mary's lips trembled and she reached for the box of hankies that sat on a side table, snatching one out.

'Where was she found?' Stewart asked.

'Outside a car showroom.'

'Which one?'

'Platinum Car Sales. They sell high-end second-hand cars.'

'I've heard of that place. In the West End.'

'Yes.'

Stewart turned to Finbar. 'Do you know where the first victim was found?'

'Yes. Superior Car Sales. Near where Platinum is.'

'And the girl we found the other day was dumped at a car sales place. Nobody made that connection.'

'The fact it was three different showrooms probably didn't jump out,' Finbar said.

Stewart looked at Mary. 'Was there anybody who Ashley didn't get along with? Any boyfriend who was giving her hassle?'

'Not that she told me. She didn't have a steady boyfriend. She'd rather go out partying in her time off. She hung out with other nurses and they had a good time. At the funeral, I spoke to one of her friends and she told me that Ashley had been hanging out with older people. People with money. She didn't elaborate.'

'On the night she died, did Ashley tell you where she was going?'

'She just said that she was going to a party at a big house and she'd be there all weekend.'

'You don't know where this was?'

'Not too far away, she said.'

Stewart asked a few more questions, but he knew he wasn't going to get any more information out of the mother. Ken came back with the tea and Finbar used the time to catch up on what else was going on in his sister's life.

They left the house and went back to the rental property.

'There's a funny smell in here,' Finbar said. 'I hope the clean-up crew got all the fucking blood off the walls.'

'He died in bed,' Stewart said. 'Yours.'

'That's it. I'm sleeping on the fucking couch.'

'Suit yourself. That's probably where he festered until he popped his clogs.'

'That's minging.'

'Christ, you're a pathologist. You take bits out of people and toss them onto a scale. You see people who are bloated when they're pulled out of the river, filled with pus. But you baulk at the idea of sleeping in a dead man's bed.'

'I didn't sleep in the bed of a bloated corpse. I'm detached from those people. This...' Finbar swept his arm around the living room. 'This is creepy.'

'Not as bad as being thrown into a refrigerated drawer or having your heid blown off in your gas-filled house.'

Finbar nodded in agreement. 'I suppose.'

Then Finbar's phone rang. 'Hello?'

'Fin, it's me, Fiona Christie.'

'Hello, Fiona. How are you feeling?'

'Like shit, but thanks for asking.'

'Where are you now?'

'I'm ready to leave the hospital. I don't want to stay here overnight. I'm scared, Fin. Do you think you could come and get me?'

'Of course. Where will you be waiting?'

'I'll watch for you. I'll wait near the taxi rank. I want to be near somebody.'

'I'll be in a police pool car. A Vauxhall.'

'Thanks, Fin. I owe you one.'

He hung up and looked at Stewart. 'That was the pathologist Fiona Christie. She's being released. She's scared out of her wits and wants me to pick her up. Do you mind if I take your car?'

'No, go ahead. If I need to go somewhere, I'll call that uniform, PC Ryan Brick laddie, and get him to come and get me.'

'What if he's off duty?'

'Then he'd better know what side his fucking bread's buttered on.' Stewart tossed the keys to Finbar, who caught them one-handed.

'I shouldn't be too long. I'll get her settled in and come back here.'

'Settled in. Is that code for give her one?'

'Aw, fuck off. She's a good looker, but we're colleagues for God's sake. Try to keep your thoughts above your tadger.'

Stewart shrugged. 'She'll be vulnerable and scared. Just don't go taking advantage of the poor woman.'

'Being a copper has certainly jaded you over the years, hasn't it?'

'I've seen it all, son. Dirty, pervy bastards of all flavours. Butter wouldn't melt in their mouths, but they have a stash of porn in the attic and a fetish for licking feet.'

'Don't worry, I won't be licking her feet or any other part of her anatomy.'

'Call me if you need me. And don't stay out too late.'

'Yes, Dad.'

Finbar left and silence descended on the old house like a thick fog. Normally on a Friday night, Stewart would be out and about, meeting up with his pals, throwing back a few beers, having a laugh.

'Is this what your life has come to, old son?' he said to himself. 'At least the old boy had a TV.'

He settled down to watch some mind-numbing pish on the box but then decided to surf the net on his phone. He didn't know how young people did this, using a little screen to find shit to look at. And the speed their thumbs went at over the virtual keyboard made them look demented. He had asked his daughter what substance she was abusing to make her type so fast, but she had merely answered, 'Fuddy-duddy.'

Platinum Car Sales. The website was half decent with photos of the cars for sale. The usual bunch were there – Mercedes, BMW, Jaguar, Range Rover, Lexus. It was who worked there that he was most interested in.

The salespeople were a mixed bag. A few men and women of all shapes and sizes, their photos taken in various stages of smiling.

It was the owner who jumped out at him. The face wasn't familiar to him but the name certainly was.

Charles Alder.

TWENTY-NINE

Finbar hated driving as a rule. He'd rather use his bike to navigate the streets, even though he came across people like Calvin Stewart behind the wheel of a death trap. Besides, this fucking car stank. God knows what they got up to in here, but there was the distinct odour of bodily functions. The house they were staying in smelled better. Maybe Stewart had let one go in the car before they left it.

He drove with the window down, hoping the cold air would rush in, disinfect whatever it was that had died, and leave behind some air that was at least halfway breathable.

The hospital was up ahead, a place he had come to dread looking at. He missed Inverness, missed his wife, missed his old life. But finding out who'd killed his niece was more important.

He saw the cabs parked in the taxi rank and looked for Fiona but couldn't see her. He pulled in behind the last taxi, leaving room for another one to pull ahead of him if the driver wanted to, then he saw the dark figure rushing towards his car. He lowered the passenger window, hoping the smell wouldn't assault her, and Fiona popped her head down to talk to him.

'Calvin, thanks for coming,' she said, smiling.

'No problem.'

'I have a favour to ask. My car is over in the car park. I need to get something from it. I didn't want to say on the phone, but I'm scared, Fin. I'm scared to even walk over there on my own. I didn't know who else to ask.'

'No problem. You're safe now.'

She hopped in and they drove to the car park, where she pointed out her car.

'Lexus? Nice,' he said.

'My ex got our other car, so I thought I'd treat myself.'

They got out and locked up the unmarked car. Fiona walked over to the big Lexus and got in behind the wheel. Finbar got in the front passenger side.

He prided himself on being an observant man when it came to doing a postmortem, but he was so focused on Fiona, he didn't notice that none of the lights came on in the car.

'I can't find it. It's a little purse. Maybe it fell under the back seat. Would you mind looking?'

Finbar opened the back door and looked down but couldn't see anything.

'Can you put the lights on?' he said, finally noticing how dark it was.

'I can't figure out what switch puts them on. I must have hit it before and now they won't come on. I'm such a dope.'

'Don't worry about it.' He fumbled about under the passenger seat, found nothing, then knelt on the rear seat and lowered himself down, swiping his hand under the driver's seat.

He didn't notice Fiona turning round. All he felt was the needle going into his neck.

THIRTY

Lynn McKenzie was sitting on her couch in what she called her 'comfy trousers': fleece jogging bottoms, but sitting in them was as close to jogging as she was ever going to get.

A glass of wine, a bowl of popcorn, a box of tissues and a chick flick on DVD. She considered herself tough, but sometimes she dreamed of having another life, one where she owned a florist and a man walked in and swept her off her feet.

She hit play, took a sip of wine, sat back – and her phone rang. She looked at the screen. Anything bar the Buchanan Galleries going on fire and she wasn't interested.

Calvin Stewart.

The last person she expected to be calling her on

a Friday night. Answer it, yes or no? She debated. What could he possibly want? She was still debating when the call went to voicemail, but he didn't leave a message.

He was going to call again, figuring she had been in the lav or something. Clearly, he didn't think she had company.

It rang again.

'If I miss this movie I have on, I'm not going to be a happy camper,' she said, hitting pause on the remote.

'Sorry to bother you, Lynn. I wanted to ask a favour.'

She rolled her eyes and sighed.

'You don't have to sigh like that. I mean, I'm not your favourite person, but trust me, I'm not the one standing behind you with a knife in his hand.'

'Sorry. Ask away, and if it isn't going to cost me money, I might consider it.'

'I need you to make a phone call and ask some-body to check on something.'

'I can do that. What do you need?'

'Have somebody who's on duty access Charles Alder. Find out anything you can about him. I know he owns a used-car dealership in the West End, and he was accused of killing three nurses ten years ago and was found not proven. I just want some more background on him.'

'Can't you ask around yourself? We're the same rank, Calvin.'

'I want to keep a low profile. Look, I know you don't owe me anything, but if something came of this, you would get the credit.'

'Okay, let me see what I can do.'

'One more thing: you haven't heard from Finbar O'Toole, have you?'

'The pathologist? No, why?'

'No reason. Thanks. Can you call me back when you hear something?'

'I will.'

He disconnected the call and Lynn held her phone for a moment. She could go back to watching her film, tell Calvin she didn't find anything and sleep soundly. But the copper in her wouldn't allow her to do that.

She made the call.

THIRTY-ONE

He had been drinking. Got carried away, got blootered, and now he couldn't remember where he was. That was the only explanation. Why else would he be sitting on a manky old wooden chair, drooling out of the side of his mouth, with his hands tied to the arms and his legs tied to the legs of the chair?

His eyes were tired, his muscles felt heavy and he thought he'd been asleep for a week. Until the needle went into his arm. Then he was buzzing as Fiona Christie stepped in front of him.

'You'll be back to normal in a few minutes,' she said.

'What are you doing?' Finbar said as he started to feel normal again.

'Protecting you from yourself,' she replied.

'What the hell does that even mean?'

'It means, you should have stopped looking into the deaths of those girls when you had the chance.'

'You know one of them was my niece?'

'Yes, that was unfortunate. I'm sorry for your loss.'

What the hell was happening here? This woman was obviously mad. Had she killed the three girls? For what reason?

'Fiona, I don't know what's going on here, but we can talk about it.'

'Classic. I like that. Try to get the killer to calm down, put the weapon away and then give herself up. Nice try, but I've seen the same films you've seen.'

'I'm not up to anything. I just want to know why you've got me here. I deserve that at least, before you despatch me like those girls. Or do you have something different planned for my demise?'

Then Fiona did something that surprised him; she smiled. 'Oh, poor Finbar. You came so close. Yet you're so very far away. Of course, you were on the right track with figuring out that the girls were murdered, just like our colleague Henry. He got suspicious and told you, so they sent him on his way to meet his maker way before his time.'

'They? Who's *they*?'

'The people who killed him.'

Finbar looked at her for a moment. 'I assumed by the way you've tied me to a chair that you killed him, just like you're about to kill me.'

'I'm not going to kill you. I just want you to stay out of the way until I finish what I started.'

'You mean *you* killed those girls?'

'Good Lord, Fin, of course not. I mean Sunshine killed them, with some help.'

'Who the hell is Sunshine?'

'The TV celebrity. He grooms young women, gives them a date rape drug, then gives them a drug that simulates a heart attack. He killed three nurses when he was living in Inverness before he went south to London.'

'That was Charles Alder. I testified against him. The verdict was not proven.'

'Charles Alder? It wasn't him. It was Sunshine.'

'What kind of a name is bloody Sunshine anyway?'

'It's his stage name. His real name is William Alder. He's Charles's brother.'

Fiona's phone dinged. She looked at it. 'Oh Christ, no.'

'What's wrong?' Finbar asked.

'I just got a notification. Sunshine died of a heart attack earlier tonight.' She looked at Finbar. 'The bastard got away with it.'

'Let me go, Fiona.'

'I can't. I have one more job to do.'

THIRTY-TWO

Lynn McKenzie pulled up in front of the house and wondered if she was at the correct address. It was in darkness and looked abandoned. Then somebody knocked on the passenger window and Calvin Stewart looked in.

'Sake, Calvin. I nearly shat myself,' she said after she'd unlocked the car and he opened the door.

'I had to make sure it was really you.'

'Who else were you expecting? Jack the Ripper?'

'That's not as funny as you think it is.' He got in the car. 'I can't get hold of Finbar. I don't know where he's got to.'

'I got the duty detective to run a background check on Alder. He has a brother, William Alder. And guess who he is?'

'Jack the Ripper.'

'You asked me for help, Calvin. Be serious.'

'Okay, who?'

'Mr Sunshine.'

Stewart looked blank. 'Who the hell is he when he's at home?'

'The TV celebrity. They come from Inverness. Finbar gave evidence in Charles's trial. He got off with not proven.'

'Finbar thinks that Charles Alder was playing games, taking off each victim's lipstick and reapplying it heavier in places so it would spell out a letter. Like he was taunting Finbar.'

'Well, let's go and talk to Charles Alder,' said Lynn.

'How do you know he's going to be at the dealership?'

'Because I called and spoke to him. They stay open late, and he's got a Bentley for sale that I'm interested in.'

'Nice one.'

'Just promise me that if I start to really get interested in it, you'll rein me in.'

'That I can't promise.'

'Why not?'

'Because I'll want to borrow it sometimes.'

'Boys and their toys.' Lynn shook her head and they headed west to where the showroom was. They chatted as they went until they got close to their destination. It was in Bearsden, a subtle building in amongst large houses.

The Bentley was sitting out front, loud and proud, under floodlights.

'He might get suspicious when we pull up in this Ford, but I told him I had come into money,' she said, parking the car.

They got out and walked into the showroom, and Charles Alder himself walked out of his office, looking very different from when he had been standing in court ten years earlier. Gone was the manky-looking toerag to be replaced by a suave businessman in an expensive suit and a Rolex.

'Aw, fuck,' Alder said, stopping still. 'Are you the bint who called me about the Bentley?'

'Me?' Lynn said. 'No, we're police officers. We can't afford to drive about in a Bentley.'

They showed their warrant cards.

Alder didn't look convinced. 'Look, I told them back then that I had nothing to do with the murders of those girls and I'm not going through it all again.'

'We just want to ask your advice on something, Charlie,' Stewart said.

'I don't give out free advice. Goodnight. Fucking time-wasters.'

Alder turned around and began to walk away, but then he heard Stewart talking on his phone.

'*Daily Record*? My name is DSup Calvin Stewart. I think you might be interested in a wee story I have about a dodgy car salesman who's selling fancy motors to upper-class customers. He's a killer.'

'Fuck's sake,' Alder said, spinning round. 'Alright, alright. What do you want?'

Stewart looked from his phone to his watch. 'I don't believe it – my watch is dead on according to the speaking clock.'

Alder shook his head.

Stewart stepped closer. 'Next call *will* be to the *Daily Record*. Stop playing games and answer a question.'

'I said I would.'

'If you didn't kill those women in Inverness, who do you think did?'

'I don't know.'

'Liar,' Lynn said. 'It was somebody close to you. They knew everything about you, your movements, where you were going to be and when, so you wouldn't have an alibi.'

'The only other person who knew things about me was my brother, William.'

'Mr Sunshine,' Lynn said.

'Yeah.'

'Were you close with him?'

'Nope,' said Alder. 'He always thought he was better than me. Always treated me like shite. He said he would come and visit me in prison. Sanctimonious bastard.'

'Where does he live?'

'With the angels.'

'What?' Stewart said.

'He died of a heart attack half an hour ago.'

'I'm sorry to hear that,' Lynn said.

Alder scoffed. 'Don't be. He was a pain in the arse. I wouldn't have been surprised if he was the one who killed those women. But he was well in with you lot back then. Friends in high places.'

'You suggesting there were dirty cops in Inverness?'

'Not suggesting. Telling you. Those bastards followed him down here. They're hangers-on. I didn't trust them because they wield so much power. Just like you two. Coming in here, throwing your weight about.'

'Nobody's throwing their weight about, Charles,' Lynn said. 'We just want to get to the truth.'

'Then go and find the truth.'

'We need your help,' Stewart said.

Alder thought about it. 'Fine. But if this comes back to bite me, I'll be calling you both.'

'Call me anytime, pal,' Stewart said. 'I don't give a shit who knows I'm onto them.'

Alder nodded. 'Let's go into my office.'

THIRTY-THREE

Sunshine dying had certainly put a damper on the weekend, that was for sure. Selfish bastard. James Mason gripped the steering wheel hard and started screaming at the top of his lungs, trying to pull the wheel out of its housing.

'Why did you have to behave like a bastard?!' he shouted. 'Why couldn't you have just told me you were taking me to London? I never would have killed you. You made me do it! I'm not taking the blame for this, oh no. You brought this on yourself.'

He put his foot down and the car glided along like it wasn't even trying.

'Christ, what the fuck am I going to do now? You were my ticket out of here, William! What in the actual name of fuck am I going to do now? Stay in that hospital for the rest of my life? I can't do that! I'm made for better things. I seriously can't do that.'

Tears were rolling down his cheeks now, blurring his eyes. He'd left Carla behind. She'd shown no interest in leaving. God knows why. The host was dead; why would she stay? YoYo knickers, that's why.

He exited the motorway and drove down a quiet street with few houses. It wasn't the best-lit place, but at least nobody would bother him here.

Except the police officers in the patrol car behind him. The strobing blue lights caught his mirror and he swore as he put his blinker on. *Fuck it.* He sniffed and wiped his nose on the sleeve of his jacket.

The uniform got out of the car and knocked on the window. Mason rolled it down.

'Been drinking tonight, sir?' the man said.

'No, I haven't.'

The officer looked puzzled. 'You okay there?'

'I just got some bad news. A friend of mine died.'

'Sorry to hear that. Would you mind stepping out of your car for me?'

'Why? What have I done?'

'Speeding, weaving all over the road. Signs of a drunk driver. I can't take your word for it, I'm afraid. I'd like you to take a breathalyser test.'

'Fine.' Mason stepped out of the car. 'Let's get this over with.'

THIRTY-FOUR

Lynn McKenzie dropped Stewart off at McInsh's rental house. Stewart was pleased to see a light was on inside.

'Thanks, Lynn. Just remember what I said about that pair of bastards.'

Lynn laughed. 'How could I forget? You remind me every five minutes.'

He waved as she pulled away. He was liking her more and more. Not that he'd ever *disliked* her, but he hadn't known if he could trust her or not. Now he knew he could.

He watched as the red taillights disappeared in the dark before walking up the pathway to the old house. He unlocked the door, stepped inside and closed the door behind him.

It was now or never.

Finbar was indeed home. He was sitting on the old settee, staring into space.

'You alright there, cock?'

Finbar looked at Stewart. 'You were right.'

'I know I was.' Stewart turned to the doorway. 'You can come out now. It's over.'

Doogie Johnson walked out of the shadows holding a shotgun. 'It's not fucking over until I say it's over. We have things to finish tonight, and you'll know when it's over because you'll be dead on the floor.'

'Come on, Doogie, don't be so dramatic.'

Johnson laughed. 'This is the way it has to end.'

'You said *we*. Your old pal Stanley been helping you out, has he?'

'Wang? He couldn't help himself out of a bath.'

'Why are you doing this?' Stewart put himself between Johnson and Finbar.

'We got in over our heads. Sunshine was going off his nut. The drugs had got to him and he started spouting off about taking us all down.'

'You were involved with him how?' Stewart asked. 'Providing security?'

'That and other things. He bent the law and we turned a blind eye. He started reminding me about how he killed those nurses up north years ago. How I was in his pocket back then. About how he killed the recent ones. Including O'Toole's niece. It was getting too dangerous. Then he goes and dies tonight. Too little too late. We'd already put things in motion. Too late to go back.'

'You called me in the other morning. Why was that?'

Johnson laughed. 'We wanted an incompetent bastard like you in charge. We knew you'd screw up the investigation and nobody would take you seriously.'

'Cheeky bastard.'

'Well, now it's come to an end. You shot O'Toole there and turned the shotgun on yourself. They'll never figure out why; they'll just assume you were off your head. Sorry, not sorry.'

'Superintendent Doogie Johnson is actually going to shoot me in the head after killing Finbar O'Toole,' Stewart scoffed.

'You think I won't?' Johnson said.

'The exact opposite. I think you will. Oh, wait, no, I don't think you can.'

'Really? You're about to find –'

Johnson's eyes went wide, and Stewart jumped

to one side and Finbar threw himself to the floor. Just in case.

'Relax,' Fiona Christie said, taking the needle out of Johnson's neck and watched as he slumped to the floor. 'He'll be asleep for a while.'

Both men stood up.

'Thank you, Doctor,' Stewart said. 'Fin called and told me what happened.'

'It's the least I could do after kidnapping him.'

'I'm glad you didn't kill Sunshine,' Finbar said.

'I was angry because he killed my sister, ten years ago in Inverness. Like the others, I thought Charles was guilty, but I knew Carol Bennet, the first victim who died of a heart attack. Henry not only told Finbar his suspicions but he told me too. I knew she had been out to the estate for a party. There was nothing I could go to the police with,' said Fiona. 'I wanted to kill him, but I don't think I could have gone through with it. I just wanted to get in his face and scream at him. I'm a doctor; I don't take lives.'

'Well, you certainly helped save ours,' Finbar said. 'It's lucky you were slim enough to hide in that airing cupboard. We'd have been well screwed if Calvin had had to hide in there.'

'Again, cheeky bastard.'

Fiona looked sheepishly at Finbar. 'I really am

sorry. I fully expect DSup Stewart to have me arrested after he deals with Johnson there.'

'Och, away and don't be daft. That stuff you injected into him – I'll tell them I sneaked up on him and knocked him to the ground. If he tells somebody about the injection, well, they've all been messing about with drugs and needles. Nobody will believe him if he says it was one of us.'

'Thank you, Finbar,' she said. 'Are you still leaving the hospital?'

'I am. I have a wife waiting in Inverness. But the night isn't over yet.'

'That's right,' Stewart said. 'I'm just waiting on the phone call to say it's over.'

THIRTY-FIVE

Lynn McKenzie felt wiped out when she pulled into her driveway. Maybe a couple of cheeky glasses of white wine would tip the balance between falling asleep and tossing and turning.

She took her key out and was inserting it into the lock when she felt a person behind her, then something being pushed into her back.

'Keep on going and you won't get hurt,' the man said.

She turned the key and pushed the door open. The man was like a second skin, he was so close.

'Don't put a light on. Get in, and if you scream, I'll smash your face in.'

'I don't do screaming. Maybe you'll be screaming in a minute.'

He laughed. 'Don't count on it.'

She heard the door being closed behind her and felt the weapon being withdrawn. Was it a baton or something else? It wasn't a knife. She was sure of that.

The house was in darkness. She had left her living room light on, but now it was off.

'Move,' the man instructed.

'What are you going to do? Inject me with a needle? Make it look like I had a heart attack?'

'You're spot on there. That's exactly how it's going to go down. Me and my dad are experts at it now. Sunshine bragged about how easy it was.'

He roughly pushed her into the living room and switched the light on. PC Ryan Brick stood looking at her.

'You're a pathetic cow, just like my dad said you were.'

'How would your dad know I'm pathetic?'

'You know who he is. He told me to get rid of you in due course. When things had quietened down. He was going to be in charge of Sunshine's security. I was going to be there with him. We were going to make a lot of money, go travelling to places I could only dream of. But Sunshine died of a heart attack tonight. Thanks to James Mason. That twat of a doctor ruined it for all of us.'

'We can have Mason arrested. You don't have to do this.'

'I already killed him. I pulled him over and gave him a dose of his own medicine. He's lying dead in his fancy car by the side of the road. Heart attack.'

'Jesus, everybody is dying of a heart attack.'

'It's the easiest way to get rid of somebody you want out of the way.' He took a syringe out of his jacket pocket. 'Like you.'

Brick took a step forward into the room and Lynn backed away towards a corner.

Then the light went out.

Brick turned round just as a torch was shone into his eyes. He didn't see the boot coming in to land on his bollocks, but he felt it. The air went out of him and he dropped the syringe as the light was put back on.

His hand reached out for the fallen syringe on the carpet, but Robbie Evans stepped forward and stood on his arm. Jimmy Dunbar smiled.

'That was a good kick, sir,' Evans said. 'And in the dark too.'

'It was, even if I do say so myself.' Dunbar looked at Lynn. 'You okay, ma'am?'

'I am. Did you get that on tape?'

'Every word.'

'Thank God you were available.'

'DSup Stewart gave us a good heads-up. Just as well you keep a spare key under the gnome outside.' Dunbar looked at Brick. 'Why didn't you think of that?'

'Who pays attention to a gnome?' Brick said, still groaning.

They saw blue lights spinning outside as patrol cars pulled up. Lynn's front door opened and Lisa McDonald walked in, followed by some uniforms.

'I suppose you got in a kick at him?' Lisa said to Dunbar.

'Dearie me, Lisa,' he replied. 'How dare you suggest I use inappropriate force? I merely used my training to disarm the miscreant.'

She gave him a wry smile and shook her head. 'Oh, by the way, I have some bad news. DCS Wang was admitted to the hospital earlier. He didn't make it.'

'Don't tell me,' Dunbar said. 'He had a heart attack.'

'How did you know?'

'It's going around.'

THIRTY-SIX

The pub was busy, but nobody bothered the small group gathered round the table. It was an old man's pub and busy for a Saturday night.

'Here's to us,' Calvin Stewart said. 'I for one am glad that Finbar is staying.'

'You're staying?' Lynn McKenzie asked Finbar.

'I am. My wife wants a change of scenery.'

'You're withdrawing your resignation?' Jimmy Dunbar said.

'No, nothing like that. I want a change of scenery too.'

'What are you going to do with yourself?' Robbie Evans asked.

'Let's just say, I've been made an offer.' Finbar looked over to the door as it opened and a big man walked in with a German Shepherd. Sparky growled at a couple of men before Muckle McInsh corrected him.

'Come on, fuck,' he said to the dog.

'That's a funny name for a dog,' an old man said.

McInsh ignored him. 'Evening, gents, ladies.' He nodded to Lisa McDonald, who smiled at him.

'I'll get you a pint, pal,' said Finbar. 'Sit yourself down.'

Finbar got up from the table and went to the bar and ordered more drinks. McInsh sat down on a chair that had been reserved for him and Stewart petted the dog.

'As you might know,' McInsh said, 'I've offered Finbar a job. He's going to be working with us as an investigator.'

'My ears are burning,' Finbar said as he came across with the first of the drinks. When they were all seated again, they raised a glass.

'To Finbar!'

The small pathologist took a beamer. 'Thanks, but it was working with the big fella here that made me think about it.'

'See? I always said you should listen to me,' Stewart said.

'We got off to a rocky start, but now we're

friends. He helped solve the murders of my niece and the other girls. Sunshine wasn't all sunshine. Sometimes he used girls and then killed them. With the help of his pal James Mason, who recruited the nurses, not only to steal the meds Sunshine needed but we suspect he fed them date rape drugs and sexually abused them. Sunshine was a real beast.'

'Thank God he's gone,' Lisa said. 'He was a real monster, preying on women like that. It's a small comfort to you, Finbar, but your sister can rest easy now.'

'She'll never get her daughter back, but yes, we know her killer is gone now.'

The evening went by fast, and as they all parted ways, Stewart stood outside the pub with Finbar.

'You can stay at my place until the insurance pays you off for your demolished house,' Stewart offered.

'That's very good of you.' Finbar slurred his words a little bit and swayed in the balanced way that only a drunk can master. 'You know, for a big bastard, you're not too bad.'

'Don't get all soppy on me now.'

'Me? Never.' Finbar clapped a hand on Stewart's shoulder. 'Come on, pal, let's get home.'

'Make them think we're a couple now, why don't

you? And get your fucking hand off me. Lisa! Tell him. He wants to come home and live with you and Liam now instead.'

'Sorry, sir. I have enough to look after.'

'Lynn. How about you?'

'Sorry, Calvin. I'm a neat freak, and you two are...well...'

'It's not me, just him.'

Lynn and Lisa linked arms as they walked ahead.

'I swear to God, if you sleepwalk...' Stewart said, but Finbar was busy with his head between two parked cars.

'Anybody,' Stewart called. 'I'll pay you. Promotions all around. Evans, you'll be inspector by Monday morning.'

'Sorry, sir.'

'He lives with his maw,' Dunbar said.

'Jimmy, come on now, I'm begging you.'

'Not even if you paid me.'

'I will pay you. Honest.'

Dunbar laughed as he hailed a taxi. 'See you on Monday, sir. Have fun.'

Stewart looked at Finbar heaving and got the boak. 'Calvin doesn't forget, mind,' he yelled at the others. But they were walking ahead and laughing.

Finbar stood before Stewart with bloodshot eyes. 'Let's go home, big guy.'

'Aye. Let's go home. I can't wait for your wife to come down here. Take you off my hands. Now you're fucking stinkin' of puke, messy bastard. You should be like me. I can hold my drink.'

'Aye, right. That reminds me, I need to change your dressing again.'

'Put your hands on me one more time, I swear to God...'

Calvin Stewart put his arm around the smaller man's shoulders to steady him. His best friend.

AFTERWORD

Calvin Stewart started life back in 2001. I had written my first detective novel by then, but I wanted to write a short story about a guy who was obnoxious, swore a lot and was hated by everybody, until he grew on them. I had been working light duties for the bus company and met some terrific drivers, one of whom stood out. I used this driver for the basis of my character. He was a funny guy and swore a lot. I wrote the story but did nothing with it – but then, years later, I slowly introduced Stewart into the Harry McNeil books, and gave him a more prominent part in two of them. And now he's taken centre stage.

I would first like to thank my copy editor, Charlie Wilson, without whom you wouldn't be reading this book right now. Once again, she stepped up when I had a problem and saved the day. Not only a fantastic editor but a truly wonderful person. Thank you from the bottom of my heart, Charlie.

Thanks to my niece, Lynn McKenzie, for being a good sport in letting me use her name for a character.

Thanks especially to Rachel Brown Hester for taking the time to share her expertise with me.

Thanks to my wife, my right hand, who is always beavering away in the background, taking care of things while I go for a journey in my head. Thanks to the other John for his advice regarding police matters. Thanks to Ruth as always. And a huge thanks to Jacqueline Beard.

Also a huge thanks to you, the reader. If I can ask you to please leave a review on Amazon or Goodreads, that would be fantastic and greatly appreciated.

Finally, in case you're wondering, the events in this book take place between *Crash and Burn* and *Dead and Buried* in the Harry McNeil series.

John Carson
New York
February 2022

Printed in Great Britain
by Amazon